Decep
Poin

When the going gets tough the men who are being hunted turn into the hunters. A young man is suspected of a crime that he denies, but he has a secret that can't be revealed. He has nothing to do with those who want to kill, but young Babbington has a secret that will turn not just his world upside down if it is revealed, but that of other people such as Betsy, young daughter of the Brand household, keeping a simple guest house catering for cowboys and travellers in the territory of Wyoming.

Will James, the hard man of the district, who has been away making his fortune, returns to find that his younger brother has been killed under mysterious circumstances – and he is prepared to kill anyone who has harmed the last remaining member of his family. When Babbington is accused of a terrible crime, only Will can help, and when one person goes on the run, hard questions are asked about the man who helps a fugitive. Deception piles on deception in a story where no one can really be trusted, even the hero.

Deception Point

Alex Frew

A Black Horse Western

ROBERT HALE

© Alex Frew 2020
First published in Great Britain in 2020

ISBN 978-0-7198-3147-8

The Crowood Press
The Stable Block
Crowood Lane
Ramsbury
Marlborough
Wiltshire SN8 2HR

www.bhwesterns.com

Robert Hale is an imprint
of The Crowood Press

Typeset by
Simon and Sons ITES Services Pvt Ltd
Printed and bound in Great Britain by
4Bind Ltd, Stevenage, SG1 2XT

INTRODUCTION

Four men rode towards the territory of Wyoming and to the county of Fremont, which all of them called home. Two of them, Tunnock and Gandon, did not look well at all.

'Reckon that yellow creek fever has got a right good hold of you two,' said their leader, an older man who looked concerned, but more for his own well-being than theirs. 'Hell, you two reprobates better not go and die on me.'

'There's been enough dying on this expedition, Grundy,' said the fourth man.

'Yep, and that's another concern, Powell,' said Grundy, who was obviously a natural leader. 'You two – Tunnock, Gandon – you boys listen to me. When you get back to Miners Delight, and your lodgings, you keep your mouths shut, you hear me?' Tunnock, who was riding low – so low that it looked as if he were praying – was kept on his horse purely by the fact that he was using a trail saddle that was designed to keep a man on the back of his steed no matter what the animal happened to do. He sat up and managed to creak his neck round, and look at the riderless sorrel travelling slightly behind him.

'We buried that mess back there,' he said. 'What's in the hills stays in the hills, and no one need speak of it again.' The words were mumbled, the fever was affecting him badly.

'Curse that little bastard Josh James,' said Gandon, sitting up too, the dullness of his long face sparking into a little fire as his mind went back to the events of just a few days before.

'That's the kind of talk we don't want,' said Grundy, 'and you boys must promise to take to your beds, recover, and don't say anything about this to anybody.'

'Makes me angry, is all,' said Gandon, 'why did the little cuss have to hang on our coat-tails like that? And why did he have to pick a fight with Powell?'

'Can it,' said Powell briefly, the man with the hand that had pulled the trigger. 'It wasn't easy and he was demanding, thought he was entitled because of who his brother was.'

'I told you, you chew it over and chew it over, but it won't make no difference to the outcome,' said Grundy. 'He joined us at the Owl Creek Mountains, far as I know it was an impulse and nobody knows he was with us. You all agree to keep it that way?'

'Can't say fairer,' said Tunnock, and the other two nodded their agreement. The five horses, one empty, rode into the open territory and through the pass that would take them to the foot of the Owl Creek Mountains and the trading post where Grundy would take his leave and hope that no one would ever discuss their adventure in the Black Hills of Dakota ever again.

*

Robbie Burns was one of the few poets that Tunnock had ever heard of. One of his famous quotes was that 'the best laid plans 'o mice and men gang aft agley.' This quaint homily may very well have served as a coda to what happened next. As per their plan to part from each other, Powell had taken off for elsewhere in the territory, while Tunnock and Gandon had ridden into town, dispensed with their mounts at the nearest livery, and departed for their respective lodgings in town.

Tunnock's landlady was a widow who took in guests and made sure that they were looked after, and she took pity on the state of her cowboy lodger, who had hinted that he would be coming back from his latest expedition with a lot more money than when he left. She put him to bed, where he went through the different stages of yellow fever, the worst being the night sweats and the deliriousness that accompanied the actual fever.

That was when things got bad for Jake Tunnock. He was in the middle of one of the night sweats when he started yelling out in his fevered sleep. Although he was up in the attic the sound of his incoherent shouting was enough to wake his landlady. Good woman that she was, she poured some cold water into a bowl and slowly climbed the stairs, holding a towel and a wash cloth across her arm. Her reasons were practical, too: she did not want him disrupting her household. She was able to put the candle she was holding in her other hand, gingerly pushed the door open, and found her lodger writhing around muttering.

She sat the candle on the bedside table, put down the bowl, soaked the cloth and put it on his forehead. He threw off the blankets and sat bolt upright with his eyes still closed. The shock of the cold cloth seemed to have revived him a little.

'It wasn't me, I tell you it wasn't. They did it – Grundy got antsy, then Powell pulled the trigger and killed the kid. It wasn't me, Josh James, Josh get away, get away, no!' He jumped out of bed nearly knocking over the candle, and scrabbled into the corner. The room was barely furnished so there was little chance of him knocking over anything else.

'I see you, I see you!' By this time his eyes were wide open, but he wasn't looking at his landlady or anything around, and his teeth were chattering.

'Now, now, you're fine Mr Tunnock,' said the landlady soothingly. She managed to get him to his feet and led him back to the bed.

'It wasn't me,' he moaned.

'Shhh,' she said soothingly, and replaced the cold cloth. She sat with him for another half hour and both the fever and his mutterings diminished until at last he fell into a troubled doze. Finally she lifted the candle and tiptoed from the room and down the stairs, fearful that every creak might arouse him again.

Although she remained calm on the outside her head was spinning. Every single person in the Territory knew of one William James, who was known as a rough rider, an adventurer, and a man who challenged those who would dole out injustice – and there was no greater injustice than the death of his younger brother.

She couldn't wait to pass on the news to a few of her select friends.

Just a few.

ONE

MURDER MOST FOUL?

Oregon Pete had a wheelwright business near the foot of the Owl Creek Mountains, and this was barely a mile from Grundy's trading post. Pete was a big lumbering man with a big lumbering mind, who was dexterous at his business of making wheels and repairing carts – and business was really good these days, with the settlers coming in and populating different parts of the territory, and needing their carts in a good state of repair. He wore a striped work shirt, over which he had flung a loose brown coat, a pair of somewhat worn trousers that had been patched in one or two places, and sturdy work boots.

His apprentice had vanished a few months before and so had Sal Grundy, and he suspected that the two things were closely connected – but Grundy had been back in these parts for more than a week now, and he would not discuss the matter in any shape or form.

The reason Pete was making his way towards the trading post was quite simple: he had developed a craving for a mouthful of whiskey, and despite the fact that he could get some tubbed gin from one of the farmers, or some rotgut beer, his hankering was for something that might leave the roof on his mouth, and only Grundy dealt in the real thing.

The trading post hove into sight and Pete pulled up his horse. It was early in the day, it must be said, and the young assistant hadn't come in yet, but it wasn't that early for Grundy, who was notorious for getting up at four in the morning and staying at the business until late, driving his various and diverse deals.

But he wouldn't be driving any deals in the near future, or indeed ever. The door to the trading post was closed, but as Oregon Pete pushed the door it opened, only for him to find there was nobody inside. It was a big log cabin, solidly built, with a small window let into each side, and then there was a big, separate storeroom nearby. The two were separated by a wide strip of grass. It was not uncommon for Grundy to be at the storeroom, but it was unusual for him to leave the store unlocked when there was no one else there. But when Pete went round the far side of the building he discovered that his old friend wouldn't be doing anything in the future because Grundy was lying on his back, dead, and not from natural causes, given that his body was riddled with bullets.

Pete, of course, immediately dropped everything he was intending to do – except, still suffering from shock, he went back into the trading post, rumbled about a little and finally discovered that bottle of whiskey he had been looking for. He took a good swig to fortify himself in body and soul, then rode off on his mount, a big black steed called Snaffle, from the noises it made, and immediately made for the lumber yard belonging to Billy Birch. Since he was working alone most of the time – he really would have to get a new apprentice – and his wife had upped sticks a few years back (and he hadn't got round to replacing her yet,) Pete needed a friend in whom to confide, and the lumber yard was midway between his own business and the trading post.

In fact there was quite a thriving community out here in the hills, and everyone knew everyone else. The yard was a place that was always open. It was where the loggers brought their trees to be stripped and made into planks, and it was the source of Pete's raw materials. The ironically named Birch – given the nature of his business – wasn't there in the open, but standing in the yard was a large man who made Pete look rather small. This was Bo Carson, who was a bit simple in the head, but who was built like one of the trees he so assiduously hauled on to the belts every day before they went through to be cut by the steam-powered buzz saw.

He was wearing a blue coverall and had on thick leather gloves to protect his hands, a battered bowler hat for his head, and large goggles that covered his eyes to protect them from flying fragments of wood.

'Say, it's old Oregon,' he said amiably, because like most big men he was good-natured. 'What you orderin' today?' He reeled back a little at the blast from Pete's breath.

'Get Billy for me, you come too, both of you got to come out to Grundy's trading post!' There must have been some urgency in his tone because Carson fetched his boss, a small, fussy man, far younger than his employee. Birch had recently inherited the business from his father. Oregon explained his position, and Birch, to give him credit, left the yard in the hands of one of his many capable workers; he got Carson to come too – muscle was always handy – and on the way out they met Eli Gantry, a widely travelled dealer in various goods, who elected to come too.

It was still early, and Grundy was in the same position between the two buildings, only by this time the assistant shopkeeper, a young man of about eighteen, had arrived. He was babbling and incoherent and obviously knew nothing of what had happened.

'Right,' said Birch, who was the organizer of the four. 'First thing we do is get him buried. We'll get a couple of shovels from his own store – can't leave him here, or the mountain lions'll get him – we'll wrap him in canvas – he's got plenty of that – and lay him low.'

'We should report this to Sheriff Palmer back in Hamilton so he can track down the killer,' said Eli.

'Sounds like the best idea,' said Carson, 'we ain't trained to track down that kind of demon.' He wasn't kidding either, he truly believed in demons and the devil himself, having been brought up that way by his tobacco-chewing God-fearing Mammy in their shack on the edge of town.

'Ain't a need for that,' said Oregon Pete, his eyes narrowing, ''cos I know the son of a hound dog what done

13

this, and we're men, we know what to do with murderin' bastards, and the store's got plenty of good, hempen rope.' Then he told them who he thought the murderer was. He was good at rousing rhetoric, and the drink had given his fevered mind a lyrical turn that spurred on the need for a quick, local response. Shortly afterwards a lynch party swung into action.

*

Betsy Brand was up and about her chores in the Brand household when Philo Babbington came back from his morning ride. It was still early in the morning.

The Brands ran a guest house along with their farming enterprise. The reason for the creation of this had been both social and economic: her father, Maxwell, had lost his dear wife a few years before to some kind of intense fever, and this had left him with four children, with Betsy, the youngest, being only ten at the time. It was a few years after the civil war, and the governor of Wyoming was offering people some good deals to come in and set up their businesses, with plenty of land on offer. His own family had arrived there before the war, and was able to see that more people were trickling into the state.

This meant that many people needed somewhere to stay while they were getting their land sorted out, and Brand senior had decided that his spacious ranch building would do the job just fine, especially as Betsy's three brothers – all of whom were grown up when their mother died – rapidly decamped to pastures new. It wasn't that they had any particular enmity towards their remaining parent, it was just that with the burgeoning railways, the gold discoveries in California, and the rapid expansion of the cities of the plains, the opportunities were there to make money and have adventures that wouldn't happen if they stayed in the rural territory of Fremont, Wyoming, where the nearest big town was Miners' Row, which contained just a few thousand people.

Betsy was left to look after the well-constructed ranch along with her father. She cooked, cleaned and looked after the guests, while her father did all the maintenance. But he was getting old – she couldn't believe he was approaching seventy – and business was slowing down, which is why he had a bright idea involving Betsy: though she was going to resist it, even though she loved the old man.

Philo came in and shook the morning rain off the shoulders of his windcheater. He was a man of just below medium height, and his green jacket gave him a deceptive bulk. He liked to wear high collars and a tie even on his day off, and he was always neat and tidy. Also, he always wore a tight, black, thin woollen cap, and had a thick, drooping moustache that hung down and partially concealed a full, almost feminine mouth.

'Enjoy your trip?' asked Betsy, standing there with her apron on.

'Can't beat a morning ride,' said Philo in his low, soft voice, that was still clear enough to carry. 'We can go a walk later if you want.'

15

'I'd like that,' said Betsy. 'Now I'll just get into this here kitchen and rustle you up some toast and scrambled eggs.'

'Thanks, that will be fine, I'll just go and change into my shoes and hang up this old thing,' said Philo, taking off his jacket. He vanished down the hall towards his room.

She was just finishing off the breakfast when her father appeared. He was a big man who wore a traditional work shirt, leather braces and old shoes. She was rather worried about him because he had grown noticeably frailer in the past couple of years, and she had to run the guest house and take care of him at the same time. In a way it was a blessing that they only had one lodger just now, and a nice, quiet man he was, too. Philo was gentle, hardworking, and just so nice to her.

'That smells real good,' said her father, taking in the aroma of the cooking food. 'I could do with some eats.'

'That's fine,' said Betsy, 'I'll just serve Philo and get you the same, won't take long.'

'Philo is it?' said the old man, 'you like him a lot, don't ya?'

'Pop, don't start again.'

'Now think about Sal Grundy, he's got a hankering for ya, and he saw ya first.'

'We've talked about this,' she said lifting the wooden tray with the plate of food for their youngish guest.

'I'm just saying, he's a mature man, with his own business. Ya would thrive out there girl, good outpost, plenty of work.'

'We'll talk about it,' said the girl in a tone that argued otherwise, before disappearing through to the dining room.

16

'Here, let me take that from you,' Philo was there and still on his feet. He looked troubled by the fact that she was serving him. He placed the tray on the table. 'Thank you very much Betsy, it smells delicious, I'll take it while it's still so hot,' Philo smiled at her. She knew that he liked to dine alone, and left the room. She went back to where her father was standing in the kitchen poking vaguely around.

'You old fool,' she said, 'who would run this place if I wasn't here?'

'Wouldn't need to,' said her father as she made his breakfast. 'Grundy, he's real well off, we could just close down the business and live off our produce – and what you can get from your husband.'

'I'm not to be sold off,' said the girl coldly.

'Grundy's comin' over real soon,' said her father, 'talk to him girl, an' see if the two of you can make a date.'

'I've already been to see him,' said Betsy, 'along with Philo, and we put him right.'

'Well, he's coming over again, and let me tell you he's a hard man to ignore, he won't give up.'

'The subject is closed,' said the girl, and made his breakfast with a little more banging and clattering than was necessary.

TWO

LYNCH MOB AND REPRIEVE

Will James was on his way to the Brand guest house. He had been up unnaturally early and he was on his way to the nearest thing he had as a home for some well-earned rest. He had been on a lucrative trip to the mid-west acting as a railway detective, had helped capture a gang who were planning to do a big robbery, and had been amply rewarded for his efforts, particularly as the leader of the gang, Brett Morrison, had been wanted for a long time by the authorities.

It had been a risky adventure but he had earned enough to live on for a while, and he was planning to take some rest, which is why he had come back to Wyoming to see his brother. Only it hadn't taken him long to find out about his brother's disappearance, and the rumours that were flying about due to the loose tongue of a gossiping landlady.

He was a big, raw-boned man without an ounce of excess flesh on his body, although he was muscular in the right places. He had a rugged face and a big chin, and women often looked at him in a certain way. The trouble was that he was restless, and couldn't always stay the course with the fairer sex, and he had never met anyone who had captured him enough to curb his restless spirit.

Mounted on his grey steed, and riding a well-worn pathway to the Brand spread, he heard the sound of horses behind him. He slowed his Shadow, his own mount, and looked back at the trail. He saw four grim-faced men coming up behind him. One of them had a thick rope curled around his arm, and he surmised at once what was happening.

'Oregon?' he recognized the wheelwright straightaway.

'Mornin',' said Pete grimly. 'So you're back, Will?'

'An astute observation,' said Will, who was not without a certain sense of humour despite the sense of gloom that enveloped him on this fine misty morning – though at least the rain had lifted. 'Where are you heading?'

'We're going to the Brand spread,' piped up Carson, unable to keep a faint tone of excitement from his voice. 'We got us a bastard to string up.'

'Why?' asked Will with just the faintest tone of disbelief in his voice.

'There's one Philo Babbington who went that bit too far in what he did,' said Birch, 'and he's gonna hang.'

'I'll get you there,' said Will, biting his lip and taking the lead.

No one objected.

*

Just a few hours previously, early in the morning when the fine spray was coming off the Owl Creek Mountains, Will James had been at Grundy's place. He knew that Sal always opened early, and that the trader would be alone because the helpmeet had to come in from town. Will also knew the questions he wanted to ask.

And he was going to get some answers.

Grundy was out at his storeroom checking his goods when a big man, a head taller, strode out of the mist cloaked in a striped poncho as a check against the weather, the wide-brimmed hat putting his face in shadow in the early twilight. Grundy was always armed with a loaded pistol tucked into his belt because marauders were not uncommon. In the early days he had even fought off Indians, but he had been a lot younger and more athletic in those days.

'What the hell do you want this early?' asked the trader, then the newcomer lifted his chin and Grundy saw that it was Will James. 'Get outta here, Will.'

'Glad you recognized me Sal, it's gonna save some introductions.'

'What do you want?'

'Guess you answered that question when you asked me to git.'

'I don't know nothing.'

'Tchh,' said Will disapprovingly, 'have you never been given grounding in English grammar? You just

20

expressed yourself in a double negative Sal, what you should have said was: "I don't know anything." Not that it would have done you a lot of good because we both know you're lying. Now let's get down to it. What happened to my brother?'

'Got nothing to tell you,' said Grundy, 'and unless you're buying you can shove on outta here.'

'I see that might be reasonable, except I heard that you were the leader of a little gold-hunting expedition, and something went wrong. Now are you going to tell me what happened, just the truth?'

'It was the others, Wesley Gandon, Rory Tunnock, Deek Powell,' sputtered the store owner, before making his biggest mistake.

Even as Will was speaking, Grundy was backing off in the clearing between the two buildings. Will, who knew the body movements of others, could see that far from co-operating, Grundy was going to try and destroy a perceived enemy. To Will the reason was simple: Grundy was simply unwilling to admit that he had been an accessory to a murder.

The trader withdrew his old army pistol, a Colt .44 from his belt, aimed straight at Will's chest and fired. Or rather he aimed at where he had seen Will, because the adventurer moved as soon as he saw the hand moving towards the gun, and was diving to one side even as the shot roared off beside him. A split second later, he would have been dead. Grundy let off several shots in a row.

'Idiot!' shouted Will, but Grundy aimed and fired again – though by this time Will had thrown aside his poncho and had twin pistols in his hands. These well worn beauties, also Colts, had saved his life more than once and he fired instinctively, most of his bullets hitting his all-too-solid target.

Even as Will strode over, Grundy was lying on his back oozing his life blood.

'Idiot!' exclaimed Will again, before getting on his horse and riding away from the scene of the débacle.

Unknown to him, he was out of there just twenty or so minutes before the arrival of Oregon Pete and his mistaken judgement.

*

The five men were nearly upon the guest house when they dismounted from their steeds and stood in front of the building. It had been constructed with much labour from local materials nearly thirty years before, and still had a rustic log cabin look even though fresh windows and a long front porch with whitewashed wooden pillars had been added in later years.

Betsy was sharp of hearing and she heard the horses coming. She went through to the dining area where Philo was finishing his meal, taking sips of his coffee.

'I don't know what's going on,' she said, 'but there's a posse out there and it seems to be led by an old friend of ours, Will James. He's been staying here in between his adventures – he likes it here.'

'Who's with him?' asked Philo carefully, dabbing at his mouth and moustache with a cloth.

'Looks like some friends of Sal Grundy,' said Betsy, a sudden fire sparked in her eyes. 'You confronted

Grundy the other day Philo, and you were out early this morning,' she looked at him with an expression that combined fondness and despair. 'You didn't do something stupid, did you?'

Philo got to his feet looking every inch the department store clerk that he was.

'I saw how he was with you, and I couldn't stand it. I went out extremely early with the intention of bearding him in his den, so to speak. I had a feeling that the warning I gave him was going to wear off.'

'Philo, do you love me?'

'That's not what it was, some jealous love-rage, I just wanted a word with the gent to put him in his place again. He's not good enough for you.'

They were interrupted by shouting from outside the building.

'Philo Babbington, come out with yer hands up or we're comin' in to get you.'

Philo was outraged: whatever he might have lacked in stature, the little clerk gained in courage. He marched straight past the girl and her father – who had just appeared when he heard the shouting – and out to the porch.

'There you are, you son of a hellish hound dog,' said Pete. 'You're gonna hang from that very porch.'

'What am I supposed to have done?' asked Philo without raising his soft voice.

'You lickspittle dog, you killed Sal Grundy, riddled him with bullets,' said Oregon Pete.

'Oh, Philo,' said Betsy, wringing her hands – the first time he had actually seen this gesture performed outside the pages of a book.

'I did not,' said Philo, 'I have not been near Grundy today at all.'

'Enough,' yelled Carson, who was holding the rope, 'get him!' The four men surged forwards: Gentry and Birch seized the clerk and pulled him on to the gravel in front of the building. Carson wrested a gun from the holster at the side of the captured man. It was a Colt like the one that would have been used for the killing, but with a pearl handle, and it looked expensive.

'Have you anything to say before I pass sentence?' said Oregon Pete, his black eyes glittering.

Then there was the sound of a shotgun being fired, not at anybody, but into the air. Everyone concerned, including Betsy, jumped at this.

'No one's gonna hang anyone from my porch,' said old Brand, 'and if they try, the next shot ain't gonna be in the air.'

'Oh, Daddy,' said Betsy, her eyes shining.

'If you want to hang the son of a bitch take him elsewhere.'

'Oh, Dad,' said Betsy in quite a different tone.

But the shot had taken effect, and all the men, including Philo, had been stilled. Into this breach stepped William James. Some men carry the unmistakeable stamp of authority, and this was the case with this impressive individual. It was the reason why he was hired for jobs involving some degree of force, and allowed him to lead men in circumstances that others would find daunting.

'Let that man go,' he said. 'I don't know him from Adam, but it seems to me you can't just drag someone

off and let him kick his heels at the end of a rope without goin' over the circumstances of his supposed crime.'

'Yes, yes that's true, listen to him,' cried Betsy.

'Hanging me without a fair trial,' said Philo, still not
raising his voice even under the circumstances.

'Set him down,' said Will, 'sit by him, and we'll go over
the evidence.' There was a tree stump nearby that made
a convenient seat, and truth be told, the morning drizzle had ceased long ago and it was turning into a warm,
pleasant day. Philo was led over to the stump where he
sat down after fastidiously wiping away some moss, and
Carson loomed over the clerk with a set expression on
his face, gun in hand in case the supposed miscreant
tried to make a break for it.

'I call forward the main witness,' said Will from the
steps of the porch where he presided like some rural
judge: 'Oregon Pete.' He already knew this was the case
from the discussion that had happened during their
trip. Pete came forwards. He was not a man who was
used to being interrogated in front of other people, and
he looked distinctly uncomfortable at being called to
account.

'I'll tell you what I know, it's a real humdinger,' he
said. ''Bout two days ago, maybe three, Betsy here and
that miscreant Philo turned up at the trading post. I
was in the back looking at some tinned goods, and they
didn't know I was there.'

'Tell the truth,' burst out Betsy, 'you were lurking in
the shadows taking it all in like some old fishwife.'

'That's fine, Betsy,' said Will, 'we'll give you a chance
to speak later.'

'Well, Betsy went up to Sal and gave him a dose of her tongue, a real sharp dose. Told him that she wasn't his and she wasn't going to be chained to some old goat, no matter what her pa said on the matter. Philo, he was there the whole time, a silent backer, kind of.'

'That's no proof of murder,' said Will.

'It's what happened after. She got real upset and rushed out 'cause Sal told her that if he had permission he would marry her if he liked, and she would see reason. This left Philo behind and he pulled out a gun, that very one and put it right under Sal's nose and informed him if he tried again to go near her, he would pay.'

'That still isn't proof,' said Will.

'Grundy's dead after them threats, that's proof enough,' retorted Pete.

'Stand down please,' said Will. 'Let's speak to the others.'

One by one the other three stood up and gave their testimony. As this went on it became abundantly clear that Birch, Gantry and Carson were very much in the mould of witnesses to the dramatic find made by Oregon Pete, and this meant at once that they were following his lead.

Betsy was asked to come down from the porch where she had stood glaring at those who would have hung Philo. She did so, looking frail and pretty in the gathering day, still looking worried and twisting her hands together.

'Betsy, I want you to tell us what actually happened.'

'Grundy came to see my father a few days ago and asked him for my hand in marriage.'

26

'Had he been courting you?'

'Yes, if you could call it that, he had taken me to a couple of dances in Miners' Delight, and we had spent some time riding together over the plains. I knew he was interested in me, and I was flattered that an older man was paying attention to me, but I never led him on and he was pleasant enough towards me.'

'So you did not really consider marriage as an option?'

'I might have, but then things changed.'

'In what way?'

'Just a few months ago Philo came to board with us, and he was so young and gentle and kind, and he made me see that I didn't want to be with an old man who wanted to own me like he owned his trading post.'

'I see,' Will looked thoughtful. 'Are you and Philo lovers?'

'No, there's never been anything like that. He likes me for who I am, he's my friend.'

'I see, and what was your father's answer to Grundy?'

'He said we should get married. We fought over that very thing.'

'Tell me what happened after that.'

'Grundy set a date when we should marry; the very same night he came and asked my father. He had already arranged for us to visit the minister in town for a civil ceremony. It was to be a very low-key affair, and I turned around and told him to get lost. Then he and papa berated me, until finally Sal walked out, promising that he would be back and I would be his wife. That's when I arranged to visit him after talking things over with Philo, who had my back, and he did.'

At last, when the evidence from the others had been heard, Will asked the smallish man on the tree stump to come forwards.

'Philo Babbington, you have been accused of murder, what do you have to say?'

'I have to say this,' the little clerk stood and looked at the men glowering at him from the far side of the clearing, then over to Betsy who was standing beside her father, 'I rode out early this morning to see Sal Grundy and give him a piece of my mind.' There was an intake of breath from Oregon Pete.

'Told you son,' he said triumphantly, 'now the confession's coming, we'll be stringin' this one up in minutes.'

'Be silent Pete,' said Will, 'you've had your chance. Go on, sir.'

'I went out, there was a drizzle coming in from the hills. There was a fair breeze blowing in my face and I was getting wet and miserable, and I thought of what I was doing. If I confronted Grundy and told him to keep away, it was going to look as if I was Betsy's lover, and there might well be a shootout – so I decided to come back. In the end it did me no good, because he's dead, and I'm not sorry. He would have turned that girl into his slave, and she deserves a lot better.'

'Thank you, Philo. Will you now sit back down?'

Will James took a stance in the middle of the clearing. He was an impressive figure, with a six-gun at each hip, and the bearing of a man who knew what he stood for. He looked directly at the lynch mob.

'You four men have put your case, but there's absolutely no evidence that this man killed Sal Grundy.

I'll agree that he might have had some reason to feel disgruntled with the man, but that doesn't make him a stone-cold killer like you're suggesting. If anything, this murder should be turned over to the sheriff. Pete, I want you to ride down to Miners' Delight and get Obadiah Palmer to come out here with his deputy and investigate, which is what you should have done in the first place.'

'Ain't gonna happen,' said Pete, who was not a small man, an ugly frown on his dark features. 'Why, this here Philo will take off as soon as we leave to report this here matter.'

'That might or might not be the case,' said Will.

'Two of us can stay here,' said Birch, 'then we can guard him.'

'Ain't no lynchers coming into my house,' said the old man. 'The boy can come in, though.' It had struck him suddenly that he was going to lose his last paying guest.

'That settles it,' said Will. 'I'll stay here with Philo, you get out of here and I'll say nothing more about your illegal necktie party, and when you come back with the sheriff we'll look into the matter again.'

Pete was disgruntled over this turn of events, but he had been hoist with his own petard.

'We'll go and get the sheriff,' he said, 'but this one,' he looked at Philo with some degree of hatred, 'he better be here when I get back.'

'I'll be here,' said Philo in his soft voice, walking over and standing beside Will. 'Look at me, am I trying to run?'

'You better not. Come on guys.' The four of them trailed off on their horses with one backward glance from the main accuser. For the sake of form Will stood there with one of his guns in his hand, but when they were gone he holstered the weapon.

'Betsy, can you rustle me up some breakfast? I've fasted for nearly twenty hours now, I could eat raw bacon.'

'I think we can do better than that,' said Betsy, in a voice that held more gratitude than she could ever express in words.

Will strode forwards with meaningful purpose, totally ignoring Philo, who spoke in a totally deflated manner.

'Aren't you going to arrest me and lock me in one of the rooms?'

'Do you want me to arrest you and lock you in one of the rooms?'

'I don't think so, Mr James.'

'Well, come inside and share a coffee with me.' He disappeared into the building and left a somewhat deflated Philo following behind, even coming up in the wake of the old man. But Philo was wearing a thoughtful expression as he went to the dining room and sat with the others.

*

In the meantime the equally deflated former lynch mob was talking to each other as they rode along. It was not a discussion filled with a great deal of *bonhomie*. In fact there might be some justification for saying that the mood of the other three towards their leader was of a somewhat hostile nature.

'You can't even get a criminal hung,' said Birch.

'There was nothing to him,' said Carson, 'he would'a choked on his scrawny neck in minutes, that's what he would'a done.'

'Will James thinks he knows it all,' confirmed Eli Gantry, 'it's thanks to him we've got to go through all this.'

'And who here invited James into the party?' asked Birch, without having to finish the accusation.

'Don't be like this,' said Oregon Pete, but he was on the back foot and he knew it. 'Once we're down there, Obadiah will take our side and make sure that there heathen clerk gets what he deserves.'

'Hell with that,' said Birch, 'I ain't admitting I was part of any lynching party. Not good fer business you see, what with some of my clients a bit prissy like and convinced that they got to go through the law fer these kind of things. I'm outta here,' he gave his employee a hard stare. 'How's about you, Carson, still want a job to go back to?'

'I guess,' and the big man cold-shouldered Oregon Pete, and rode behind the already departing Birch.

'That leaves the two of us,' said Pete.

'Not really,' said Gantry, 'I left my samples at Grundy's.'

'What samples?'

'I travel in soap, real good scented soap bars for the ladies, industrial green soap for cleaning in shops and factories, and fancy soaps in all shapes and sizes for decoration. I was hoping to get a good sale in the green stuff from Grundy. I get paid a commission, and I thought this was going to take an hour out of my day, get to see an interesting hanging – give me a story for bar nights in the city – and instead it's winding up complicated. Upshot is – see you around Pete, if you ever need any soap that is,' and with this parting shot Gantry rode off in the direction of the trading post.

Cursing under his breath Pete kept a fixed course. He was in a mind to give up, but in his own head Philo Babbington had taken on the shape of a minor demon that had to be exorcised, and he, Pete, had the means to do so. With fixity of purpose he headed towards Miners' Delight, or the former Hamilton City, to visit the sheriff who would eventually see that the little clerk got the come-uppance he deserved for shooting a friend of the wheelwright.

*

Will James was going through several agonies of indecision. Not that he showed this while he was eating his well-earned breakfast. The trial and the subsequent dismissal of the lynch mob had been an exercise in restraint for the adventurer because throughout the whole event not one person had seen the elephant in the room. Why was Will James himself on the trail early that morning, and what had *he* been doing when Grundy was killed? The fact that he had a reason for killing the trader – being shot at was a reasonable defence – did not take away from the fact that some hard questions should have been asked.

He did not want to raise the matter either, for a very good reason. If he confessed to the killing the matter would be investigated and he would be jailed until the trial. He was an innocent man, who had been attacked and acted in self-defence, and he was pretty certain that his defence would go over – but he wanted to find the man who had killed his brother, and he was pretty certain that once Powell knew Will James was around he would skip town, and fast.

Another factor that worried Will was the behaviour of Philo, the clerk. Most people if they were accused of a crime would become upset, angry and in some cases quite tearful, but the truth was that Philo had remained calm throughout, except for showing a reasonable denial.

As they sat in the back dining room drinking coffee, he looked over the young clerk.

'Who are you, Philo?' The clerk, who was finishing his milky coffee, looked at the man who had saved his life with big, dark eyes.

'I'm not sure what you're asking,' he said. Betsy, who was hovering nearby, gave Will a look of reproof.

'Leave Philo alone, if he says he's done nothing wrong, I believe him.' Will looked at her slightly flushed cheeks and gave a knowing smile.

'Betsy, let the man speak for himself, I'm just trying to get some answers before the sheriff arrives. People are always suspicious of strangers; I'm just trying to get to know our friend here.'

'I've been travelling about the state,' said Philo. 'I came from Cheyenne. Some of my skills involve clerical work, so I got a job with Folger's department store in town. I don't have a place of my own, so when I heard Brand took in guests I came here.'

'You have a strange, kinda high voice, and you wear that stretched cap all the time,' said Will. 'You're quiet and sparky at the same time, as you showed when you put a gun to Sal's face and warned him off.'

'I don't have to explain myself to you,' said Philo, who looked as if he was going to get up and walk out of the room. A look from Betsy quelled this desire. 'All right, stranger, if you must know, I had an accident when I was young and it crushed my throat – we were playing with a tree swing and I hit a branch. My Adams apple never developed properly, leaving me with this voice. As for my head, I wear this cap because I have a condition where my hair grows in patches and leaves me bald in others on my scalp. It's unsightly, so I would rather have it this way. That's the biography, and I'm not going to say any more.'

'There are a few other questions,' but Will had drained his own cup and eaten a breakfast big enough to fill a small army. 'However, let's wait until later, I'm going for a nap now, it'll be at least two hours before the sheriff gets here and I intend to make the most of them.' He looked at Philo, who was still sitting, with Betsy hovering behind him looking anxious. 'Now will you give me your word you won't try to escape?'

'I won't try,' said the lodger.

'That's good enough for me,' said Will vanishing to his usual room and leaving behind the astonished pair.

THREE

IN SEARCH OF JUSTICE

Hamilton City, Fremont County, was a medium-sized town that had arisen in this part of Wyoming for many reasons. It was in a fertile part of the country, the land was fed with rich minerals by the rivers that came down from the Owl Creek Mountains, so that left plenty of scope for farming and ranching. The area was rich in various minerals including iron, silver and coal, so there was plenty of scope for mining, and the climate was reasonably temperate although the rains could sweep down for days at a time and the snow could pile high in the winter.

As Oregon Pete rode into town he saw a prosperous community with a main street that contained many modern stores and eating joints. There was nothing that could be described as a high class restaurant, but there was the very department store, Dulse and Greys, in which Philo Babbington was employed to do his clerical duties.

Midway down the main street – which was wide, as main streets tended to be in this part of the world, mainly for the passage of cattle drives and ease of goods transport – was the sheriff's office, which incorporated the local jail. It was a large, solid building that stood out from its surroundings because it was made of solid brick, with a few steps leading up to a wooden porch and a slope to either side that led to the boardwalk.

Pete already knew that the sheriff had two deputies, and that Obadiah Palmer was what they called a hard-ass who looked on the killing of prominent citizens as a major blight on the community. Luckily it was still early on in the day and he was able to catch Palmer just as he was coming out of the building. The sheriff knew Pete well because he was always using the wheelwright for on-the spot repairs to the county's coach or other vehicles owned by the county.

'How do Pete?' asked Palmer, 'looks as if you're on a bit of a push today. Got a job on?' The sheriff was a big, benevolent-looking man who had a solid look about him as if he might be made of clay, so if you were to cut right through one of his limbs it would show the same pasty colour all the way through. He had a shock of greying hair that showed at the edges of his brown hat, and carried a holstered gun in his bullet belt. He wore a loose, dark green shirt and black trousers and his leather boots were slightly dusty as befitted a man who patrolled his own streets.

'It's Sal Grundy, he's dead,' said Pete. 'I found the body. Philo Babbington did it.' Then he proceeded to tell the whole story, carefully editing the part where he had led a lynch mob to take revenge, turning them instead into a bunch of concerned citizens. 'So, Will James, who we met on the trail, is with him right now. You need to come out and arrest Babbington and take him in for trial.' Pete was not a man who concealed his emotions, so his story, told outdoors, had already reached the ears of several passers-by, thereby ensuring it would be spread throughout town.

There was no need for one of the men to hear the gossip second-hand. As Pete went into the sheriff's office – Palmer would need extra weapons, handcuffs and other accoutrements to affect an arrest – Rory Tunnock, who had been walking nearby, took in everything that was said. He was pale and thin, having just recovered from his recent illness. He had been going out to look for work, but now he hurried away for a different reason.

He had to go and visit Wesley Gandon.

*

In the meantime Will James slept as if he were never going to wake up, doing so for a solid two hours. He woke up feeling quite happy with life and well refreshed, and went to see the titular master of the house, who was sitting in a rocking chair on the porch.

'Maxwell, I got to get going. Just to ask, do you know where Philo went when he headed out?'

'Philo? Oh he's still here.'

'What? Well, I got to say, I was intendin' to stay for a while, but I got a little task to do – though I can't let you lose out because I've changed my mind and I intend to get going.' He drew out a stack of dollars. 'I'll pay you for a week.'

'That's mighty good of you, but I couldn't take your money,' said the old man.

'I'd feel better if you did. I don't rightly know when I'll be coming back.' The old man looked at him shrewdly.

'Personal business, eh, not unconnected with this mess?'

'Yep, I guess you could say that. Tell you what, take this as a deposit and take it off my board against my next visit.' This time the old man took the money and tucked it into the front pocket of his overall.

'That's mighty neighbourly of ya, friend. I'll take yer money on that basis.'

'I have to move on,' said Will. They shook hands and he departed. Truth told, he knew that by having his sleep he had not left them much time to get away – and in his mind he used the word 'them' with a purpose.

He found that Philo and Betsy were still together. They had obviously been talking with each other, and Philo was looking unhappy and stubborn.

'Right, get your things together,' said Will, addressing the clerk. 'We're moving out right now.'

'I'm not going anywhere,' said Philo in that strange voice. 'Let the sheriff take me.'

'The sheriff should not arrest you,' said Will, 'it's obvious that you're not the only suspect in this – mess.'

'And what about my job, they're expecting me back at work tomorrow?'

'Well, you know what, you ain't going to be doing any clerking from a prison cell, that ain't the usual arrangement.'

'But you said the sheriff won't arrest me.'

'"Won't" and "shouldn't" are two different things. The sheriff trusts the word of Oregon Pete, and he is liable to lock up a suspect just as soon as look at them. He likes to have a suspect because it makes him look good, and the truth is they wouldn't be that fussy about putting you on trial as long as they get somebody.'

'He's right,' said Betsy, 'and Grundy was popular 'cause of his position, supplier to those going into the mountains and on the trail.'

'He was about to marry this delightful young woman,' said James, 'and even if you don't care about yourself, think about Betsy here. I've stayed here for years, on and off, and she's one of the best girls I know. You can't drag her through this.' As he was saying this he was acutely aware that time was flying past on swift wings.

'He's right,' said Betsy. 'If Obadiah doesn't investigate properly I'll be dragged into this affair – he might even arrest me as a guilty party in it.'

'It's what these here people call an "accessory after the fact", but if you're gone then he'll be too busy tracking you down and he'll forget about the girl. He has a one-track mind, does our sheriff.'

'And will he track me down?'

'You'll be with me,' said Will simply.

This seemed to be the turning point in the conversation. Philo got up and went off to pack, coming back a short while later with a bag full of goods, and wearing his windcheater. Packing in such a quick time was a male trait, thought Will.

'I've got some money,' said Philo. 'I won't say goodbye to your father, but I've left a week's rent on the table.' Betsy came forwards, and without warning grabbed Philo and hugged him close. Philo struggled with this and pulled away, while Betsy stepped back with an odd look on her face.

'I won't let you down,' said Betsy. 'They won't learn a thing.' Then she put her hand to her face and vanished into another part of the building.

There was very little conversation between the two oddly contrasting men as they went out to the stable, saddled up their horses and packed their goods. Will observed that Philo was extremely dexterous at filling his saddle bag, and ready to go in minutes. Whatever else he was, the clerk was efficient, and not a bad horseman either, so it wasn't long before they were riding out together and into an uncertain future.

*

Just about ten minutes later Oregon Pete and Obadiah Palmer arrived at the Brand house. It was empty of visitors now, so the word 'guest' was no longer a suitable appellation for the building. It wasn't long before the two men were facing up to Betsy and her father in the neat and tidy front room. The older man was not one to be questioned: as far as he was concerned he knew both his guests well and he liked them both. On the other hand he now had an unmarried daughter who was going to remain that way for the near future, so he just remained silent.

'I know nothing,' he said. 'I'm blind and deaf to it all, I wasn't up and I didn't even see Philo come back from his mornin' ride. That's all you'll get out of me.'

'Then I need to talk to *you*, Betsy,' said Palmer. 'Explain to me what happened between the three of you – Philo, Sal and you.'

'She ain't going to tell you the truth,' exploded Oregon Pete. The sheriff looked at him with a cold eye.

'Seems like I made a mistake. Pete, get outside and cool your heels on the porch. I want to hear what this young lady has to say, unpolluted, as it were, by your presence.' Pete muttered a few words under his breath that should not be said out loud in mixed company, and went outside.

'Now that he's gone,' said Palmer, with deceptive gentleness, 'tell me what happened.'

Betsy explained about the fact that Grundy was determined to marry her even against her wishes, and that Philo had simply backed her up and showed that he meant business, and how he had gone for a morning ride to warn Grundy off, but had changed his mind.

'How long was he out for?'

'About twenty minutes.'

'That's fine,' said the sheriff.

Then she explained how Pete had found the body and brought the lynch party to this very place. It might

41

have been expected that Palmer would have been somewhat surprised that Oregon Pete had not been leading the party of concerned citizens, as he had intimated in his earlier conversation, but Palmer showed no surprise whatsoever at this turn of events. He knew Pete to be a man of uncertain character.

'So who was in this little gathering?' he asked.

'Leaving out Pete, there was Billy Birch, Bo Carson and Eli Gantry. Oh, and there was a regular guest of ours that they met on the way.'

'Say, what's this guest called?'

'Will James, he comes here when he's in the area because he visits his brother.' Then the girl paused and looked as if she did not know what to say, 'All right, you're the sheriff, you're going to know this, you know what goes on in your own county. Josh James has disappeared and Will could be here for that very reason. I'm not stupid enough to ignore that fact.'

'So we have the intervention of a man who is trying to find out what happened to his brother?'

'He stopped Philo from being hanged. That was what he did.'

'Then the two of them rode off into the woodlands? Maybe they know each other and the death of Grundy was a put-up job?' Betty shook her head fiercely.

'I swear, Will has been away for over half a year, and Philo just showed up a couple of months ago. They've never met each other.'

'Hmm, that's something that's up for questioning,' said the sheriff, but more to himself than the girl. He got busily to his feet, but being overweight he grunted a little. 'That's all for now, Betsy, you're a good girl. Now I have to get Pete and go, we've got a lot of riding to do, because we've got to go and look at the body.'

'That sounds like a good idea,' said the girl. 'So do you suspect Philo?' The sheriff looked at her shrewdly.

'I don't suppose it'll do any harm, and it'll help me form my thoughts. Philo, well he's the least of my suspects. First on my list is Pete – he found the body and he's still stinking of whiskey. Maybe, just maybe, he riddled the trader with a few bullets and took what he wanted. They didn't always see eye to eye. He told me on the way here that they buried the body to keep it from the mountain lions, but they could have taken it indoors and wrapped it in burlap until I arrived. Seems to me the first person who finds a dead body, well, he or she might be the one who created that dead body.'

'And what about Will?' asked Betsy, 'he doesn't go around randomly murdering people.'

'Will James lost his brother – and Grundy financed an expedition that Josh James went on,' said the sheriff. 'Josh disappeared on that expedition, and they said he went into the hills. I had to accept their explanation because that's what they said. Now it don't look so clear cut. I got to tell you, Will James is a survivor, he knows this area better than any man or woman alive, and he can shoot a coney at a hundred yards. He's what I would call a great woodsman who has spent time with the Injuns, he can track down and kill a man with his bare hands, but if he's fired at he can shoot better than anyone I know. Good-day, young lady.'

The sheriff put on his hat and departed.

43

FOUR

AN IMPOSSIBLE DILEMMA

A man walked into town, his sorrel walking beside him as he led it by the reins. He had the look of a person who was used to going from town to town. He wore a black shirt and blue jeans of a superior cloth to basic work trousers, and a well-cut jacket in a lighter shade of blue than his trousers. Around his neck was a black string tie. He led the horse to the livery and left it in the capable hands of the keeper there, and then went into the town itself.

There was something of the predator in the way he moved, looking around all the time, watching the different people he met on the way. Hamilton was a bustling town with many going about their business, and one or two women smiled at him, because he was a good-looking man.

He came to The Three Barrels saloon and went inside, up to the bar, and ordered a double whiskey;

then he looked around. The clientèle were mostly male, and he showed no interest in them whatsoever.

'Penny for 'em?' said the barman. 'I haven't seen you before, stranger.' He had already noted that the new-comer was armed with a Smith & Wesson revolver at his hip, stuck into his belt.

'Just hittin' town,' said the stranger, 'looking around, see what's happening.'

'Name's Joe,' said the barman. 'What's yours?' the stranger turned and gazed at him, and looked as if he was actually thinking about his own name.

'Name of Troy Walker, stranger,' he said, then turning the idea of 'stranger' on its head, he shook hands with Joe and gave a smile that showed off his good teeth, but which made him look a little wolfish. Joe suddenly had a thought that this was a man who had an aim, he couldn't say why, except that the stranger had an air of purpose that did not sit well with his attitude of being an aimless drinker.

'So do you know a lot of people around here?' asked Walker, throwing off the question with a seemingly casual air.

'I guess,' said the barman, polishing a glass with a none-too-white cloth. 'What do you want to know?'

'Would you know any women who stay around here?' The barman's smile broadened – he thought he was getting a fix on what his visitor wanted.

'Girlies? Sure, I can introduce you to someone who'll give you a good time, there's one or two in here even.'

'Not that,' said Walker, 'maybe some other time,' and he gave the barman the name of a particular woman. Joe shook his head, 'Never heard tell of that one.'

'Well, thanks anyway,' said Walker, downing his whiskey.

'Another?' asked Joe.

'No thanks,' said Walker. 'Just one thing, do you have a game going at night, poker preferably?'

'We do,' said Joe, 'though it can be pretty high stakes – some of these ranchers, they got good money and they like the thrill of the game.'

'High stakes is what I like,' said Walker, turning away. 'See you sometime, got a lot of places to visit.' He jammed on his hat as he parted the batwing doors with an air of barely suppressed fury, and the attitude of a man who had a lot to do and not enough time to do it.

*

In another saloon not far away called The Brass Keys, Tunnock staggered in looking rather like a ghost and saw Wesley Gandon sitting there on a chair at a table in the corner. This particular hostelry was a bit rougher than the one just frequented by Walker, since it was the place miners would gather just after work. It was really no more than a room in which to drink or play cards, with natural light coming in through narrow windows to illuminate a sawdust-covered floor, and creaking chairs that would have been discarded by any reputable owners. It was well known that the barman hid a loaded shotgun behind the bar, but the worst thing was that sometimes he had to use it. But the drink was cheap and it was a place to find work.

'I thought I'd find you here, your favourite hell-hole when you retreat from life.' Gandon gazed at Tunnock in a hazy manner, betraying that his acquaintance with the rotgut on offer was at an advanced stage.

'What do you want, you bastard?' he asked, which was not exactly an encouraging greeting.

'I've got news for you, I hurried here to tell you.'

'What?'

'Sal Grundy's dead.'

'Is he?' Gandon had a bottle and a glass in front of him; he poured another drink but pointedly did not offer anything to Tunnock.

'He died of a hail.'

'Bad weather?' hazarded the former explorer.

'No, a hail of bullets, he was cut down by a person or persons unknown, though they say someone called Philo Babbington did the deed.'

'Him?' Gandon swallowed some of his whiskey. 'I've met that one, he works over at the new department store further into town. He's a little guy who goes about his business and doesn't bother anyone.'

'That's not the news, I don't believe it either, but Oregon Pete's been down here to fetch the sheriff, and he mentioned that Will James was guarding this Babbington to make sure he didn't escape.' Gandon was sitting there as if suddenly frozen into a statue of himself, the glass approaching his lips. He set it down again, and his eyes took on a haunted look.

'So Will James is around and he ain't the suspect?'

'We know better, don't we Wesley?'

'I guess we do,' said Gandon.

'What are we going to do?' Gandon picked up his glass and downed the whiskey with one gulp.

'You always did lack a bit of imagination,' said Gandon. 'Me, I'm going to finish this rotgut, go home and sleep it off. You, I would advise to go and look for a job on one of the ranches, sleep in a bunkhouse with fifteen or twenty other men, because we both know what's going to happen next. Once I'm sober I'm out of town, I'll head for Laramie or even out of the territory altogether.'

'I guess that's the best idea,' said Tunnock.

'You bet it is.' Then the both of them jumped as a man came into the saloon and looked around in a purposeful manner before striding over to the bar and starting to question the barman. The new arrival was smooth-looking and wore what Tunnock would have called gambling gear, if the latter had not been so nervous.

'Walker,' said Gandon. 'Ain't seen him for a while.'

'I thought for a moment it was Will James.'

'Don't bother with *him*; he's a good long ride away from town. Now get, leave me alone and I don't want to see you again.'

'Thanks,' said Tunnock. He left the saloon and headed straight for his lodgings, where he kept his gun. He could barely afford the bullets, but he would have to make do, because he had no other choice.

*

Will was not an easy taskmaster. He knew that other parts of Wyoming were not heavily forested, so he led his companion through forest trails that he knew well, but others might never have seen. Nor did they make it easy on the horses, travelling a distance of some forty or so miles and ending up at a higher point of the Owl Creek River where there was some degree of shelter from the elements, and even a few caves if they had to abandon their horses and escape from a posse.

To Philo's credit, the clerk showed an unexpected skill in riding that Will would not really have expected from a pen pusher.

Finally they dismounted and went to a spot where the horses could rest and crop grass while the riders sat down to get their breath back. It was a glade beside the river, with a low rocky outcrop where they could sit while the horses were grazing. They took their saddles off and wiped them down with a cloth to remove excess sweat, because when the animals stood still beside running water, sweat could cool down and give them a chill. They also checked that the banks there were low enough for them to drink. Once more the clerk saw to this without being prompted to do so by his companion, causing Will to raise his eyebrows.

Finally they were able to sit with each other and eat some of the bread and cheese that Betsy had provided for them. The clerk turned away as he ate, pulling up his moustache with his forefinger, taking dainty bites of the bread as he did so. Will finished first since it had become his habit to eat quickly. The kind of life he led was not conducive to sitting down and eating long, hearty meals that made him sleepy.

'I don't get you,' he said to Philo when the clerk had finally finished his food.

'In what way?'

'I knew that idjit Pete would take ages to ride into town and come back with the sheriff because he would try and persuade his pals, and one by one they would refuse to come with them, then he would sulk about it for an hour before deciding to do the right thing. I also knew I would need some sleep because of an early rise – a real early rise – and so you had two hours to escape.'

'That's right.'

'My point is, why didn't you?' Now they were sitting close to each other Philo looked at the traveller with big dark eyes.

'I knew I was innocent. That was good enough for me.'

'Trust me, around here being innocent ain't as good an excuse as you think.'

'I didn't speak to you about this, not having time, but thank you for intervening in my capture and possible subsequent lynching.'

'That's the most roundabout way I ever heard of being thanked for saving a life.'

'What are you planning to do now?'

'I'm going to take you in any direction that leads you out of Wyoming.'

'Then what?'

'Oh, I'm staying around here, I have a lot of business to conduct and I won't be quitting until that business is done.'

'You do realize that I might have planted a bullet in Sal Grundy's head if someone else hadn't beaten me to the punch?'

'Why?'

'He confronted Betsy in his store one day after her father had sent her there for supplies, and he grabbed her and twisted her arms and pulled her hair and told her she was going to be his wife whether she wanted it or not. And that senile old fool of a father approved of the match!'

'Is that the reason why you went back that time?'

'Betsy is a fine girl; she shouldn't be made to marry someone just to save her father from bankruptcy, especially when they could have a working farm. The old fool – her father – was just being lazy.'

'It seems to me that your interest in Betsy is just a little more than friendship, as if you were warning another man off her.'

'Well, mister, that's just where you're wrong. Women aren't a man's property, not around here, but Grundy hadn't cottoned on to that fact yet. Besides, I know all about him – he was married before, you know.'

'Who told you this?'

'I work in a department store, its great the gossip you get to hear, although I don't take part. It seems that his first wife was no more than a glorified slave, who died in childbirth. That was the only way she could get away from his bullying. His second wife…'

'Whoah, back up stranger. Second wife? What in the ringin' of hell's bells do you mean?'

'That's what I'm saying, his second wife ran off about seven years ago with a traveller who supplied Grundy's trading post. She was reported missing, presumed dead. I think she's missing all right, the kind of missing where she's living happily in the city with her five children and the traveller.'

51

'That puts a whole new spin on what you've been telling me.'

'Grundy was rich from selling spades and supplies to would-be miners, but he was as mean and horrible as any man could be. He would have ruined Betsy's life.'

'I think I'm starting to understand what riled you up so good.' Will looked at the young clerk. 'Another thing about you puzzles me – you ride real good for someone who works in a store.'

'I guess. You see, I grew up around these parts – further out towards the cattle district. This part's more farming, I would say.'

'You were undersized to become a cowboy and clever enough to write up ledgers and letters, so you eventually took yourself off and got a job in the nearest town in the new store?'

'That just about sums it up, and the town's a bit of a distance from the Brand house, but I don't mind, it's good exercise for Farthing – that's my horse – and I like the work and being amongst the young ladies who work in the store.'

'Well, you can't go back to work, that's a dead cert. I guess if we get you to the wilderness, we can get you over to Colorado in a couple of days. They're always looking for people like you over there, who ain't that interested in mining or logging or that kind of physical work – your skills should get you a job real quick.'

'I'm not leaving Wyoming.' Philo gave him a direct look.

'If you go to Johnson, Carbon, Jeffrey City, Lander, or any other place around here, you'll be one of those refugees who have fled because they've done something wrong. They'll cotton on to where you are, eventually, and fetch you back to Hamilton. Truth is, Grundy was well off and well known, so when someone like that dies, then they have to find a scapegoat, and that'll be you.'

'I didn't kill him,' said Philo sincerely.

'We get that, but you go in front of one of them juries that have been gathered for a circuit court, with a mean judge in an area like this, and they'll string you up faster than Oregon Pete would on a good day.'

'You know what? I agree with you Will, but that doesn't mean I'm going to flee from here like a hysterical schoolgirl. I'm going back,' said Philo, and from the tone of his voice Will knew he was on a losing streak.

Inside he knew that he was dealing with an innocent man and wanted to protect him, but he also knew that he had to get back to town and seek the men who had either killed his brother or allowed him to die, and he also knew that with the sheriff on his tail he didn't have much time to complete his task.

He was faced with an impossible dilemma.

FIVE

THE TRUTH REVEALED

Wesley Gandon came out of The Brass Keys and headed for his own lodgings. He, too, was beginning to run out of money, and he felt bitter about the expedition that had lost him so much. Despite the whiskey that he had imbibed he felt more tired than drunk, which was good because he would soon rest and chase away the restless thoughts that kept chasing around his head. He wasn't a killer by nature, and he hadn't liked what Powell had done to the young man during his argument. Like many, he had hoped that time, distance and a new job would allow him to forget what had happened, and move on with his life.

That was when he met Eli Gantry in Main Street. The two men knew each other vaguely because Gantry had been around when Grundy was arranging his ill-fated expedition. Grundy considered the traveller to be a long streak of nonsense who talked the talk but who was a conjurer of falsehoods, and who had helped him to fund and lead the most ill-fated expedition since Custer's attempt to suppress the Indians at Little Bighorn.

'Hello Wesley, haven't seen you since Sal came back from his wee trip,' said Gantry.

'Eli,' said Gandon, 'what a surprise.' He started to walk on, but it was obvious that Gantry was a man whose nerves had been considerably jangled, and who needed to talk to someone with common knowledge of the situation.

'I'm glad we met. I suppose you heard about Sal being murdered?'

'I guess,' said Gandon. 'He always was a contentious cuss. Guess his past caught up with him.' He was rooted to the spot for at least fifteen minutes while Gantry told him about the lynch party and the intervention of Will James. 'I've been thinking about this since coming back to town,' said Gantry, 'and I think Will is the real party behind this – it just never occurred to me before. His brother disappeared on the expedition, you know – Grundy hinted that he went off on his own, but I met Josh in the yard, and he was a weak kid. He wouldn't have gone off on his own. Something happened when he was with Grundy – say, you were there, can you tell me?'

Talk about giving a man enough rope to hang himself.

'Nope,' said Gandon, feeling this was a weak response.

'Do you want to go for a drink?' asked Gantry. Normally Gandon would have jumped at this offer with the kind of alacrity shown by a starving wolf offered a fresh steak, but the news of what had really happened had penetrated his brain with fresh urgency.

'Gotta go, Eli,' he said. 'Some other time,' and he hurried off – as much as he could hurry in his present condition. The salesman looked after the departing man and knew that he was the possessor of knowledge, true knowledge.

*

Tunnock was back at his lodgings, packing some of his meagre possessions into a cloth bag – spare boots, coat and pants, along with a picture of his mother and one or two things he had picked up on his travels. He was going to do exactly what he had been told: he would try to get a job on one of the ranches outside town, or he would go to Riverton and get work down one of the mines nearby. He would like to see Will James get him when he was five hundred feet underground.

That was when he heard the thunderous knock at the front door of the building.

The knock of doom.

It wasn't a casual visitor, he knew that for a fact, as no one ever called at this time of day; most of those who lived here worked in town for many hours and sometimes into the early evening.

He knew that he had been ill, and that he had only just recovered, so there was some excuse for the fact that he had not left sooner. Unlike most of the others he had actually known Will James before the ill-fated trip that led to the demise of Will's brother; and he also knew that James was not the kind of man to forgive such a blow to his family, and that he would deal summary justice at will, paying very little heed to the law of the land. But Tunnock knew he should have packed sooner, in fact as soon as he heard Oregon Pete talking to Obadiah Palmer.

He took out a large brown slicker that he had used in the past when he was a rider, a job that he had been hoping to get away from for life. The attic window was stiff, barely being opened during winter, spring or summer, but at last he levered it open, tied his bag to a rope – cattlemen always had rope lying around – and lowered it to the ground.

He squashed his hat low down on his head and ran down the stairs at a speed that, if he slipped, would send him to the bottom and break his neck. Basically he was trying to beat his landlady to the punch. If he got down first there was a chance he would get out of the back door, grab his things, get to the livery, fetch his steed and ride off before James – assuming it was James at the front door – even knew he was gone.

Just as he got to the bottom landing the landlady sailed out of her kitchen – she loved her kitchen – and opened the front door to the shadowy figure waiting outside.

If there had ever been a time for Rory Tunnock to have a heart attack, this was it, but he was too busy trying to get through to the kitchen where the back door was inconveniently situated. He was just vanishing in that direction, ignoring the startled cries of his landlady, when he heard a familiar voice – and it was not the one he dreaded.

'Rory, why are you in that get-up? We got to talk.' It was Gandon.

Minutes later they were back in the attic, the only place where he could get any kind of privacy. There had been a slight delay while he went outside and fetched his bag, beneath the wondering gaze of the landlady, who looked as if she was having serious doubts regarding his sanity.

'I didn't really worry about what you were saying,' said Gandon, sitting on the bed while Tunnock took the only other seat in the room, a creaky old chair. 'I thought if Grundy was dead that would be it, but you know what the truth is? Will James was part of a lynch party and managed to get them to break up.'

'I tried to tell you that.'

'But the way he handled everything, made them go away, Eli Gantry told me how he did it, he ordered them around like he was something special and had nothing to hide. We know different, don't we? We both know he's the killer.'

'That's a fact, no one would believe it outright, but we both know some little clerk ain't going to take out Grundy.'

'I got to thinking that we need to get out of town,' said Gandon, 'pool our resources, like.'

'Sure, sure,' said Tunnock eagerly, 'if we go to one of the ranches we're bound to get some work real soon – I've got friends in the Cattle Association, and once I use their names we'll get places.' He realized that his friend was looking at him in a manner that indicated some degree of pity.

'Listen to me: we have to face up to this danger. I ain't even heard what happened with that sheriff, but I bet you that Will James made that clerk, Philo, go with him – James, I mean – and depart for pastures new. They'll be well out of the reach of the law. James knows this territory better than any man alive.'

'What do you mean?'

'If I was him I would make sure that before I did anything I would have a hostage. That's what that Philo will be.'

'Makes no difference to us, does it? All we need to do is get our gear together and get jobs, like I said.'

Gandon rolled his eyes in despair.

'Listen to the man, I know Will James, I've spent time with him. He's a demented sucker, once he gets on the track of a man he won't give up until he gets him. If we run we're dead men, it's not like we got money, we can't jump on a train and flee to the other side of the country.'

'What do you want us to do?'

'Easy, I suggest that we get our weapons together – we have a couple of guns and a rifle between us, and we ride up into the hills and look for the man.'

'Can I suggest to you that seems a little bit mad, Wesley?'

'That's the point, the whole thing is mad.'

'But you just said that he'll have taken off? Do you really think he would try to get us when the law's on his tail?'

'I do, and I can tell you, having a hostage puts him in a real powerful position. We've been riders, we can go into the hills, live under a bit of canvas, track him down instead of the other way round, and make sure he doesn't do to us what he did to Grundy.' For the first time in a while Rory Tunnock felt a wave of relief flooding over him. To be the hunter rather than the hunted made him feel a great deal better.

'And once we've dealt with our little – problem – we can look for work?' asked Tunnock.

'That's a given,' said Gandon. 'Once we've done this we'll be off in different directions and never talk of this again.'

'Suits me,' said Tunnock. 'No time like the present.'

*

Will was in a dilemma. He knew that he had to get back to Fremont County soon or his prey might well vanish. He also knew that the sheriff was not a stupid man and might work out that Will was after certain people. However, he felt responsible for the clerk.

The day wore on and they soon found a sheltered cove near the water. In winter this would be a flooded area as the waters came down, but those very waters had worn a natural cavern into the side of the rocks. At night, with a woven guard made of thin branches and a blanket at the entrance, this would be a safe and warm place for the travellers. He had decided that they could spare one night and he conveyed his decision to Philo.

'I'll catch some food, light a fire, and we'll rest here for the night to let 'em get used to the idea I won't be hunting 'em, then you'll stay here and I'll return.'

'And what is my role in this, pray?' asked the clerk.

'You'll wait another day, and if I don't come back you'll take off as we agreed, go find yourself a job in Colorado or another county. By that time they'll know you've got nothing to do with what happened to Grundy.'

'All right, I'll help you set up camp.'

They were both armed with broad, sharp knives for general work, and they used these for cutting brushwood and piling it up to help conceal the entrance to the low cave, also using the same type of brushwood for the fire. They both laboured at their task in silence, and brought back their respective loads and dumped them nearby.

He noticed right away that the amount of brushwood Philo brought was significantly less than his, and that the clerk was struggling to cut some of the thicker branches, slicing at them a little ineffectively. He began to suspect that the reasons for him becoming a clerk were more to do with his strength than anything else – he would simply not have had enough physical prowess and stamina to rope and herd cattle.

At last, when Will deemed that they had enough materials, they looked at the barrier they had built in front of the cave.

'That should keep out the mountain lions and other attackers,' said Will, 'and once we hang a horse blanket on the inside it'll help keep out most of the chill. It can get real cold here overnight, with us being at the foot of the mountains.'

'I've worked up a bit of a sweat here,' said Philo, 'I'm going off to find a sheltered spot and have a wash and change this shirt.'

'Don't matter where you bathe,' said Will, 'creek's right across there, cast off your duds and knock yourself out, son.'

'No, that's not going to happen,' said Philo. 'I want a little thing called privacy.' He gathered up a change of clothes, and moved off with a kind of quiet dignity, his moustache bristling a little.

'Fancy city notions,' said Will, shaking his head. He made a fire with the expertise of a man who had done the same thing many times in his life. His trap had caught a couple of rabbits, and he expertly prepared these and put them on a spit over the flames. Spending time with the Indians (for whom he felt a great amity) had taught him he could find green plants that could be harvested and eaten with the meat, so he gathered some of these, too.

He gauged the time that it would take Philo to have his wash, and decided, based on what he would have done, that the other would be nearly finished. The meat was cooking so he decided to go off in search of the clerk, and maybe throw a pebble or two to startle him. Male nudity was no issue with those who had been cattlemen and who had shared their lives, bathing in rivers whenever they had the chance.

Philo had moved quite a distance, actually going round a bend in the river before entering the water, and was at an inlet sheltered by tall reeds. Will stooped, picked up a couple of pebbles with the aim of throwing them beside the clerk and startling him.

He parted the reeds, but what he saw startled him so much that he stood like a statue, his mouth falling open, the pebbles staying in his hand unheeded, never to be thrown.

*

Deek Powell was at the trading post at the foot of the Owl Creek Mountains. He was a tall, thin man who wore a permanently gloomy expression on his sallow features. His clothes were in dull shades of blue and grey, and his boots were of plain leather. He was there when Obadiah Palmer arrived with Oregon Pete to investigate the death of the owner.

'Hi – the assistant storekeeper brought me up to date,' he said. 'Can't believe Sal's gone, knowed him since I were a kid.'

'Seems nothing's news in this county,' grumbled Palmer. He turned to Pete: 'Now it's your job to show me his mortal remains – seems to me you'll have to bring a spade. Show me where you found the body, too, before you dragged him away.'

'You don't believe me?' asked Pete.

'Listen, you reported a crime, and murder's a serious business, and whoever did this deserves to hang,' said the sheriff. 'You all right, Powell?' He said this because the thin man had turned noticeably paler and gulped audibly.

'Nothin' sheriff, just real distressed about the death of an old friend.'

'Well, Will James and a little clerk are in the picture right now,' said the sheriff, 'but if you know anythin' better you can let us know.'

'Mind if I tag along?' asked Powell, and anyone listening could have sworn that there was a trace of fear in his voice. He followed the two men as Pete showed Palmer the clearing where he had discovered the body. 'So where is James?' he asked casually.

'Will James is halfway to Montana, if he has any sense,' said Palmer, 'no point in his staying around here if he's guilty of anything. It's not as if there's anything that might give him a reason to stay around, some special knowledge. Now let's see the body.' He turned away, and failed to see that Deek turned even paler if possible, and swayed a little, like a thin tree in a high wind.

Oregon Pete grumbled for a while, but he recruited the young boy who had formerly worked for Sal, and Deek. The body had been buried in a shallow grave, which meant that it didn't take them too long to uncover the canvas below.

'Take him inside and unwrap him,' said Palmer. He had not been keeping still – while they were at work he had directed Pete to show him where the body had been found originally, lying between the trading post and the storehouse. He had carefully examined the sides of both buildings. He came inside a minute later and found Sal lying on his own counter, intact except for the rather obvious wounds on his body.

'One, two, three, four bullet wounds,' said the sheriff, counting aloud thoughtfully. He got the others to hold the body on its side. 'Yep, four bullet wounds, two of 'em pretty close to the heart, the others lower down, probably because he shifted position.' He stopped examining the body.

'So who does the store go to?'

'I think he has relatives in Cheyanne,' said the boy, who was barely seventeen. 'I guess I'll have to close up and go tell them. At least he had his own hoss and cart.' He didn't look happy at the thought, mainly because the territory between towns could be dangerous for a lone traveller.

'So we think we know the murderer?' asked Deek eagerly, 'sure could have been Will James, he's a wanted man? Will I get the posters printed up?'

'See, there's a problem with that,' the sheriff held out his right hand, palm upwards, displaying a flattened bullet. 'This is from a colt .44, I recognize it – now what kind of gun do you use, Pete?'

'Smith & Wesson,' said that gentleman.

'And you, Deek?'

'I ain't got a gun any more,' said Powell, 'lost it on our little trip – I mean I lost it, under duress, a-whiles ago. I got a Winchester right now. Different bullet, right?'

'Right, but this is a lot more, because it's a bullet from a particular type of Colt, the old army model, I know that much. So what gun did Sal use?'

'I found his gun nearby,' said Oregon, 'I brought it in and left it by the counter.'

'Right, where is it?' asked the sheriff. He took the weapon and looked at the gun closely. 'Couple of things here: this has been fired recently – you can tell if you look at the barrel – and this is an older type bullet.'

'I don't get it,' said Pete.

'This wasn't a clear-cut case of someone being attacked and killed: it looks as if Sal did a bit of firing of his own. The store had chips on it where it was hit by bullets and I found this one embedded. There was a fight, and it looks as if he lost.'

'What are you saying?' asked Deek.

'Looks to me as if this ain't clear cut,' said the sheriff. 'There's a possibility it wasn't murder.'

SIX

A WOMAN'S RIGHTS

Will did not stay where he was, instead he went back to the makeshift camp they had created over the last couple of hours, and made sure that the food was cooked. He served it on the tin plates that he always carried – sleeping out had never been a problem to him since he was a young man. It was one of the reasons he had always stayed ahead of the world, a form of self-reliance in which he asked for nothing from any man – or woman.

Philo came back looking rather subdued, but seemed delighted the food was ready. He thanked Will and went off to another part of the clearing.

'I like to eat alone,' he said.

'No bother to me,' said Will, 'do as you please.'

Philo came back after a short while and returned his plate, which Will dipped in the river and cleaned with some broad green leaves, along with his own.

They sat in a fairly companionable silence drinking their coffee, then Will threw away the grounds of his drink and stood up, moved back and faced the clerk.

'Sometimes people see me, and they think I don't have a sense of humour,' he said, with a quirky grin. 'But you know what? The odd time I like to sneak up on folks and startle 'em. While the food was cookin' I planned to do that to you, sneak up on you while you was bathin' and splash a few pebbles around you and startle your prissy ass.' At his words Philo looked up sharply, started to rise, thought better of the matter, and sank down again. 'So what's the moustache made of?'

'Horse hair, from the tail,' said Philo in a subdued voice, higher than the one 'he' normally affected.

'That's why you eat elsewhere, ain't it?' asked Will. 'The steam from the food melts the glue sometimes and makes it slip a little, ain't that the way?'

'Yes,' said the clerk. 'So you saw?'

'Not all the way down, but enough to tell me that you ain't what you've been telling everyone. So what do you use to stick the moustache on? I guess it ain't horse-hoof glue or you'd never be able to get it off.'

'I use spirit gum from the store.' Gingerly Philo eased the moustache off her upper lip, revealing a shapely mouth that would have given her away immediately. She pulled off the cap and let her long, brunette hair fall down to the shoulders of her slim body. Will had thought of the clerk as being somewhat underdeveloped, but now he realized that 'slim' was exactly the right word. Now he knew why she always wore an ill-fitting striped shirt that was baggy below as well as above, and also why she didn't like taking her jacket off. From what he had seen when he was peering through the reeds the top half was not badly endowed in a womanly sense.

'What's your name?' he asked. 'OK, I'll set the ball rolling: my name is Will James and I suppose I'm what you would call a free spirit. I run off and work wherever I can make a living and come back – or used to come back – to make sure my brother is doing well.' He did not add the words 'though not any more,' to this, but there was a sense that the words were there.

'I'm Pauline Ryder,' said the girl, 'daughter of Bart Ryder of the territory of Wyoming.'

'Then why the heck are you living here as some guy – quite a good disguise, by the way – and not on your father's ranch?'

'It's not his ranch any more, it's mine.'

'Surely that would be even more reason for you to stay, rather than run and hide and pretend you were someone else? For that matter, why dress as a guy?'

'The truth is, I knew that I was going to be tracked down, and I wanted a disguise that would prevent me from being discovered as a woman. Changing my name just wasn't enough.'

'I'm surprised you got away with it as long as you did.'

'The world is an odd place – people often interpret things the way they want to interpret them, and part of that interpretative process lies in believing what we are told. Most people tell the truth, you know, in a broad sense, and besides telling my employers and the Brands that I was a man with a few health issues, I didn't lie about anything else,' she sighed. 'I got a lot out of working in that store, it made me feel normal, writing up the sales ledgers and the letters. I'll miss it.'

'You still haven't explained why you were on the run – did you kill someone?'

'No, precisely the opposite Will, someone was trying to run me into the ground and destroy me.'

'And who would that have been?'

'My husband.'

*

The man sat at the back of Hamilton Baptist church and waited for the rest of the congregation to file in. He had arrived here early for precisely that purpose. Like most of these communities, the church was an important institution in Hamilton, and everyone who could attend, did. He was a good-looking man with a mop of slicked-back black hair, a straight nose, a firm jaw, and piercing blue eyes that stood out even in the subdued lighting that came through the plain glass of the tall church windows behind him. (For reasons of cost and taste the Baptists tended not to go for stained glass.)

The man was sitting far enough along the back, burnished wooden pew that he could view each person as they entered the building. He did not show any emotion on his tanned features as the church filled up, but one or two women looked at him in a frank manner, even though they were accompanied by their husbands, and he could tell they would be quite happy to converse with him at the church social afterwards. He would be equally happy to do this at some point. But as the actual church service started and the Rev J. Johnson Jones began assuring the assembled congregation that they were inevitably going to hell, taking a long time to tell them so, the man got to his feet and slipped out of the side door as silently as he had arrived.

This was not to be a day of rest. He had another three churches to visit, where most of the population of Hamilton City would be at this time of the morning, and he was not going to stop until he had visited all three. Troy Walker was on a quest, and he wasn't going to rest until he was satisfied that he had explored every avenue – and found the woman he wanted.

*

'Your what?' The girl, on inspection, did not look that old, but there was a tradition out here of women marrying young, so on reflection the idea was not that surprising.

'What happened was that I had two brothers, both older than me. Our ranch is fairly big and it's situated just outside Riverton. My father built up the business and managed to make it profitable. But tragedy struck – one of my brothers was driving cattle to the Oregon trail when he was ambushed by Indians and murdered by those heathens.' Will did not like her attitude to the Indians, but it was pointless arguing with her and reminding her that this was originally their land.

'My other brother got in a bar fight in Riverton one night just over two years ago and was shot dead. That meant that I would become the sole heir of the Ryder spread when my father died.'

71

'So what happened?'

'Troy Walker was what happened,' said the girl. She paused, her eyes gazing into the distance as the memories returned. For a moment she did not speak, as if it were too painful to discuss, then she made an inward decision and the words came tumbling out. 'Troy had done some work for my father in the past, negotiating with cattle agents and so on. He was – is – a tall, handsome man, with the best smile you've ever seen and deep blue eyes. He's a really good-looking man and he became interested in me.'

'Funny that, just after you became your father's heir.'

'It was like a whirlwind, you know, and I was well caught up. He took me to dances in Riverton, out drinking with some of his friends, and riding in the hills. He was older than me and so attentive and courteous I felt like a lady for the first time in my life.'

'Hell, I know his sort,' said Will gruffly, 'the charm offensive. I've met that kind many times in my life. They take some poor, innocent girl who's been brought up isolated, and press her into liking them with their weasel words and their pretend attention, just for gain.'

'What? It sounds as if you know him!' For a moment the young woman looked stricken, almost as if she was going to cry, then she gathered her resolve and stiffened her features.

'If I had only known, but what's the use going down that path? The problem wasn't just him making up to me. I guess if it had just been us I would have seen through his intentions, but Pop loved him. Pop saw in him a solution to all his problems, because with the best will in the world, Pop thought a woman couldn't really run the business when he was gone. So I married Troy. Yes I did, in the Baptist Church in Riverton, and with my one remaining relative to give me away – my father.' She dabbed her eyes.

'At first I was happy, but even at the wedding I had seen that my father was faltering, he was so glad I was finally "settled" as he called it. He was ill, and he had hidden it from me, and when he couldn't hide it any more he took to his bed and died.'

'Let me guess,' said Will, slowly and with a degree of analysis that was surprising to the girl. 'Your father didn't change the will.' The girl flashed a look at him that contained, to his surprise, more than a trace of triumph.

'I'm glad he didn't change his will, because it meant that I inherited the property, lock stock and cattle.'

Will felt as if his head was going to start aching as he tried to figure out where all of this was going.

'Is that at all a good thing? Surely as your husband, Troy Walker gets your money and your property anyway, ain't that the truth?' The girl looked at him appraisingly.

'You would think so, but the truth is that Wyoming is not like most of the states in this old-fashioned country. For a start, a lot of the immigrants around here come from Scandinavian countries, where women's rights are a great deal more advanced than most places in the world – and for another the government, starting in the fifties, wanted to encourage more women to settle out here, so the laws are liberal – and women have the vote and inheritance rights.'

'Now that's something I've never really thought about,' said Will.

'You wouldn't, would you? This is usually a man's world,' said the girl, 'but in this case I hold all cards. I own what I own, and that's that.'

'Well, that still don't explain why you're parading around in those duds making like you're some kind of freaky guy,' said Will. 'I'm missing some kind of connection here.'

'Sure you do,' said the girl. 'I was still in mourning for my father, old Bart; Mom had died a while ago, long before my brothers, so that meant I was in no fit state to run things. So Troy did what he needed to do, and got the hands to look after the horses and the cattle and get the place in some kind of order, made sure they were paid on time, and even hired a book-keeper to make sure things didn't fall behind.'

'Wait, I know your spread!' said Will. 'The Ryders, you've got a lotta land and thousands of cattle; I thought I recognized the name. You're well off, so what in the name of Satan's boots is goin' on here?'

'Troy came to me about two months after father died and asked me for money. I pointed out that he was living a good life on the ranch and that the money would be sorted out in due course. Then he confessed – he had been raiding the coffers and going out gambling when I thought he was doing business. He had mismanaged funds, and hiring the book-keeper had just been his way of finding out exactly what assets we had.'

'You argued with him?'

'I told him he was no husband of mine, not with the way he was behaving, and he hit me for the first time. I was still depressed and confused, and he kept berating me and wanting me to hand everything over to him. So I went to my chief hand, Burrows, and put the ranch in trust to him – and I disappeared.'

'Why?'

'Because I knew that if Troy did not get what he wanted he was going to hurt or even kill me – and I refused to sign anything over to him. He would fake my name on documents and I was prepared to renounce him, and any feelings I had for him died the moment he struck me. What's wrong?' She stopped speaking, because Will was red in the face and his fists were clenched.

'I was married once, and I never touched her once in the wrong way,' he said, 'and any man who treats a woman the way your husband treated you, needs to go and meet his maker at the wrong end of a bullet.'

'It's why I disappeared. I needed respite from the whole existence into which I had been trapped, and I had the money because I had my own bank account. That was three months ago.'

'You haven't been back?' The girl looked at him defiantly, and then her shoulders drooped.

'I guess something happened inside my head. Once people accepted I was just some slightly odd little clerk they left me alone. You've no idea how good that felt. All my life I've been something to somebody. I used to be Mummy's little daughter, then when she died I was Daddy's, then as I got older I was an object of desire for men. Then I just had to get married because I was not fit to be an heir because I was female. So I came here, lived with Betsy and her father, and just got on with life. I kept telling myself it was time to go back and face up to my responsibilities, but as time went on I slipped into a different way of life.' She gave her head a bitter shake. 'I guess that's why I was so set on defending Betsy.'

'Those men would have hanged you, yet not once did you call out what you were, that would have settled the whole thing,' said James.

'Maybe, but I was in no frame of mind at the time to shout my business from the rooftops. Besides, when they started they would have found out, but when you began that mock trial I decided to hang on for as long as I could manage.'

'What're you going to do now?' The girl shifted uneasily and got to her feet.

'It's been a long, tiring day, and I think I should sleep on what's happened, don't you?' she went to the entrance of their makeshift shelter. 'Let's see if this blanket keeps out as much of the cold as you claim.'

*

Will sat beside the fire for a long time, wondering what he was going to do. He didn't want to tell the girl that he had killed Grundy. He had many reasons for doing this, the first being that if he told her, she would become his accomplice, and he wanted her to remain his 'victim' in the eyes of the law. In addition he could see now that she had been protecting the woman, Betsy, who had become her friend.

Mostly he was experiencing a kind of inner rage. He had to get back to the area around Miners' Delight – which was the name most people used for Hamilton City. When they had ridden to this place at the foot of the mountains he had considered in his mind that he was helping an innocent man escape. In a sense he had wasted a lot of time, but he knew that his actions would allow the situation to cool down.

The area around the trading post at the foot of Owl Creek was spacious and heavily wooded, not like the wide open, sometimes arid plains to the south. He had meant to guide Philo Babbington to a safe trail – as safe as anything could be for a lone traveller in these parts – and plan his comeback accordingly.

Now he couldn't see why the girl should come back with him all the way. Instead he would persuade her to take action and regain her old life.

It looked to him as if she had no other choice.

The ashes of the fire were getting low. He was a smoker and had made several roll-ups, smoking them thoughtfully as he sat there. He stamped out his last smoke and went to the shelter, pulling aside brushwood. They had piled up plant life and laid coverings on top of this to soften their backs, and he had laid out his bedroll, which he always carried with him. The girl had taken this, so he resigned himself to sheltering under the remaining horse blanket.

As he entered and replaced the brushwood at the entrance in front of the fast fading light outside, the girl gave a moan and sat up, looking at him with real fear; but this faded rapidly as she saw who it was.

'Bed down,' he said gruffly, 'your virtue's safe with me.' Truth was, it had been a long day and the gunfight that had started things off at six in the morning seemed a very long way away, as if it had happened months, not hours before.

He was nearly asleep, in that twilight between the real world and the realm of dreams, when he felt someone roll over and come close to him, and an arm that went over his chest. It was an approach for nothing other than comfort, and although he went rigid for a moment at the touch he said nothing, and soon drifted off – but just before sleeping he heard a small voice:

'You're a good man, Will James.'

He wasn't so sure on that score.

SEVEN

THE NOOSE
TIGHTENS

Troy Walker was feeling frustrated. He had been through all the churches in town that Sunday and hadn't seen his wife. Of course going to church was not compulsory, and it could well be that the fear of being spotted was enough to keep her in her lodgings, wherever those were. But his day wasn't finished with his visits to the religious establishments: that night he went out to the best saloon in town and engaged in a game of poker with local landowners. This was where he was in his element, pretending to knock back large amounts of alcohol (watered down by arrangement with the barman, while deliberately getting the other players drunk), and handling the cards adroitly; but after the game, in the course of which he won quite a few dollars, he departed for a back room where he had arranged to meet an old friend.

The two men shook hands; the man he was facing was in his mid-thirties and was smaller and a great deal less handsome than Troy Walker. He was dressed in less finery than his would-be employer – a sober, dark green lounge suit, a cream shirt and a dark brown tie. He had wavy fair hair and a face that was serious in repose, but lit up when he smiled.

'Huck Wilder,' said Walker. 'I didn't think I would need you so soon.'

'Sure is good to be wanted,' said Huck, with a trace of humour.

'My wife has disappeared,' said Walker, 'and I know enough about you that you would be able to do the business for me, take my place, and do what's needed.'

'What did the poor sow do to you?' asked Wilder.

'I married her, that's what she did to me, but you knew that already,' said Walker, with a slightly sour expression. 'She was all right, but too fawning, like a lot of the bitches. The big problem was, I wanted to get my hands on her ranch, truth being that a woman ain't fit to run a business, they don't have the concentration us men have, or the experience.' But Huck Wilder was looking at him in a shrewd manner.

'You married her to get your hands on her property and sell it to the highest bidder.'

'Never mind that, and cuss the government! When this benighted territory was set up they made a mistake and said that a woman has as many rights as a man – as if women would even properly understand what that means.'

'Where do you come from?' asked Wilder thoughtfully.

'I'm Texas, born and bred,' said Walker proudly.

'I had an inkling that's where you hailed from,' said Wilder, 'so when you came through to here, you kind of thought that things were the same, and they're not, so it means that when you married and the old man shuffled off his mortal coil, like, you were going to get everything automatically – and you didn't.'

'She vanished, but I know women, they like some kind of security,' said Walker. He took out a picture of the woman they were discussing and handed it to Huck. Even in black and white it showed her good side. Huck gave a low whistle.

'Not bad, wouldn't you be better sticking with that one and making a few little Walkers?'

'She ain't my type, I like 'em big and blonde and fun. Mite too serious and responsible, she was – besides, she would try the patience of a saint, all moody and crying over her old man hopping it to heaven. No, she's not a bit of use.' His manner became brisker. 'Her father had interests in this town, which is why I think she's around here, holding on to the bank book and the securities that really belong to her husband. I want you to track her down, and once you do, leave her wallowing in her own ignorance. Then contact me and we'll make sure we do the business – only you pull the trigger while I'm elsewhere getting an alibi.'

Wilder sucked in his lower lip thoughtfully. 'How much?'

'I'll pay you a thousand dollars.' To show he meant business he took out a bundle of notes that he had managed to earn that night. 'Here's a hundred dollars for your expenses to show I put my money out there.'

'I still don't understand why you want her dead.'

'There's no chance of us reconciling, I wouldn't stoop to beg a woman,' said Walker coldly. 'If she'd given me what I wanted, things would've been fine, but she crossed a line when she behaved like she did, and she'll never be my woman. When she's gone I'll get what's hers, every building, every fence, every goddammed cow and every bank account she's stashed her fortune in, because I'm the husband.' He began to move towards the door. 'You just get in touch when you find her, that's your job, and we'll get her to a place where she'll never bother me again. If you get the opportunity you might even want to finish the task there and then…' he shrugged '…doesn't bother me.'

'Where are you going?' asked Wilder as his new employer opened the door.

'Back to the ranch, where I'll be the distraught husband still worried about the disappearance of his wife. They don't even treat me right there – that head hand, Burrows, once this is all over he's getting sacked, but he holds all the cards right now because she handed him power of attorney over the ranch right before she vanished and made it all legal, like, with her lawyer – little bitch has a lawyer, would you believe it? I ride out first thing in the morning. 'Til then,' he gave a wicked grin, 'Bella's goin' to entertain me upstairs and tire me out.' He strode off, leaving behind an investigator who thought that if Pauline Ryder didn't want to see her husband again, maybe she was making the right choice.

He looked at the photograph once more, studying the contours of her features. Shop to shop would be his first line, because unless this woman was a hermit she would have to buy food and other necessities, and Hamilton wasn't that big a place.

Troy Walker might lack the patience to seek her out properly, but a thousand dollars was a lot of money. Huck smiled again as he slipped the photograph into his breast pocket. He was on to some good earnings here. He slipped out of a side door so that no one in the saloon would see him – it wouldn't do to make an obvious connection between him and his new employer, not when so much was at stake.

His grin broadened as he went into the street. A thousand dollars was fine, but he would get rich, when, after the necessary was done, he blackmailed Troy Walker for a great deal more.

*

For once in his life Will James was not the first person to rise in the morning. He was awakened by the noise of someone singing softly to themselves, the crackle of a burning fire, and the smell of frying bacon. There really was nothing to beat a fried breakfast. He came out of the cave and found a bright-eyed girl sitting there, the Philo cap and shirt back on, cooking their meal.

'Smells good,' he said.

'You do what you have to do and I'll get yours ready after I eat,' she said. He joined her shortly thereafter and she kept her promise, preparing the coffee while he ate the hot food.

Neither of them argued about what was happening that day. He would go out of his way to make sure that she was in her own territory, and then he would leave her and go back to the area around Owl Creek to find the killers of his brother. He was aware that she was looking at him sharply.

'What's going on with you Will?'

'I don't know what you mean.'

'You're a clever, able and hard-working man. Look at this shelter: you constructed it with the help of a sharp knife, your hands and your brain. You're capable, is what I'm saying, yet you're roving around the territory like a lost soul. You're searching for something.'

'Say, time's getting on,' he dumped his coffee grounds and swilled his mug in the river. 'Supplies are running out and we got a long day ahead.' He stood up, a tall, raw-boned man with a weathered face, but a strong jaw and an expression of fierce determination.

'All right, I understand you don't want to talk about it. You're like my father, one of those old-fashioned men who think it's not a woman's business.' Now she was faintly annoyed with him, which disconcerted him. He was only trying to protect her from the truth about what had happened to Grundy. He did not understand women, which was possibly why he had lost his wife to another man. The girl went off to make her preparations and came back a short while later with her cap on, wearing the moustache, and with a cowboy hat jammed down low over her head. This, along with the old clothes, transformed her back into the clerk that she had been. He looked at her with disapproval.

'I thought you were finished with all that carry-on, Miss Ryder.'

'I'm Pauline, as you well know – after you protecting me I think we're on first name terms – but while we're out here I'm Philo, the gun-ready clerk and the suspect in the Grundy killing.'

'I don't see the point if you've decided to go back.' But then he thought about the matter, and concluded 'But I guess it's safer for us both. A woman is a target out here, for all sorts of reasons. Too many see her as an easy prey.'

'If they saw me like that they'd have a slug in them before they could lay a finger on me – or anything else,' said the girl.

They loaded the saddlebags, put the horse blankets on their steeds, saddled them and put on the load, got on them and started their long trip.

They had ridden a long way, but Will wasn't too troubled by this. In a way it had given them a respite while they were considering what they had to do, and it had led to a revelation concerning his companion that had changed events for ever.

It was such a distance that they had to stop halfway, eat, and see to their bodily needs. The landscape had changed now. Will, who had travelled these trails many times, had made a change in their course so they were heading towards Riverton, and the outskirts of the Ryder spread. The sun was hot, so the rest in the shadow of a clump of cottonwood trees had done them a lot of good, and they were careful to allow the horses a long drink of water.

'Won't be long until you're on your way,' he said. He wondered at that point, was there some trace of regret in his own voice? Was he getting attached to having a companion? He dismissed the thought from his mind – he was a lone wolf, and that was the way it was always going to be.

They were getting closer to the ranch when they heard a horse coming up behind them, and saw a big chestnut quarter horse catching them up along the trail. The rider was a man in dark clothes, which must have made him hot and bothered in the hot weather, and even when he was in the distance the girl gave a gasp of recognition.

'Don't let him know it's me,' she said, 'it's my husband.' Few people were out there in the rising heat, and it was a matter of simple courtesy that travellers always greeted each other.

'How do?' asked the tall, good-looking man sweeping a glance over the dusty travellers. 'Heading my way?'

'We're going to Riverton,' said Will, instinctively speaking for the two. Will became aware that Pauline's hand was twitching towards the gun at her side, and he kicked the flanks of his own horse with the heel of his boots and moved forwards to conceal what she was doing. At the same time he gave her a warning look and she became more subdued, but he had a sense of what she wanted to do.

'I'll ride along with you, I could do with the company,' the new arrival swept a look over Will's companion, but there was no recognition on his handsome features. 'Your friend's not saying much.'

'He's had a throat infection,' said Will easily, showing a verve for invention that surprised even the liar beside him, 'he can't talk just now.'

'I can come with you so far,' said the stranger. 'Got to get back to my ranch. The old Ryder spread, you heard of it?'

'Sure, it's a big one,' said Will.

'Far as I'm concerned it's a pain in the rear. I'm Walker. My wife, she's gone, presumed dead. I'm glad; I would strangle the little bitch. She's not right in the head, acted up with me, all scenes and fighting and keeping a man's legal rights from him.'

'My name's Will,' said James. 'We've been riding a distance, we'll be slow.'

'Well, sun's getting up, my horse is fresher than yours, guess I'll make tracks,' said Walker. He stared briefly at them both, gave a nod, and headed on his way, whipping up the animal to make it go faster and soon disappearing into the distance.

'Why the hell did you let him go?' asked the girl, 'I was just about to hold him up and take him prisoner.' Even in this extreme she held to her principles and would not kill the man she no longer thought of as her husband.

'Then what?' asked Will James.

'We would hold him prisoner and I could claim my rights,' said the girl.

'That wouldn't have worked,' said Will, 'you're already a suspect in a murder dressed like that, and you'd've had to reveal who you were to the sheriff of Riverton. He might have put up a fight, and he's a big, strong man, there's a chance one or both of us could have been killed.' But his strong face took on a look of concern.

'You can't go back now, he's clearly not going to give in without a fight. Come with me and I'll get you shelter and we'll deal with him soon, together, but not yet, not while I have things to deal with.'

'What things?' asked the girl, her fake moustache bristling, but he had already picked up his reins and was spurring his horse onwards.

*

Huck Wilder was as good as his word. He went around the town of Hamilton with the photograph encased in his leather wallet, because it rained regularly around these parts and if it got wet he wouldn't be able to get another. Photos were expensive, and this one would have cost the formerly happy couple real money.

He went from one shop to another and showed the precious picture to all he found there, but saying it was in confidence to those with whom he spoke. He knew there would be a lot of gossip from those wondering who the girl was, but that didn't bother him – by the time anyone wanted to seek him out, he would be out of town.

His patience was rewarded in the early afternoon of the second day when he went into Dulse and Greys, the new department store. He was impressed by the size of the new store and the variety of goods on offer.

Hamilton must be doing well, he thought, as he looked around.

In a sense the store was also a reflection of the more enlightened equality laws of the territory. It was a place where women could meet because it had its own café where they could have long chats, talking about their men and putting the world to rights, and enriching the store owners by consuming copious amounts of coffee and cake.

Huck walked through his surroundings feeling somewhat out of place, pretending to look for the men's clothing. He saw a couple of pretty girls behind a glass counter that displayed necklaces in silver and gold, while others were decorated with pearls. He stopped his pretend search and gravitated towards the young women. They were well dressed and giggled as he approached, obviously thinking that he was going to make up to them.

'Good afternoon, ladies,' he said, sweeping off his hat and bowing a little. This made them giggle even more.

'How can we help you?' asked the saucier of the girls, a buxom young lady with red lips, whom his mother would have called a 'scarlet'.

'Why, seeing such beauty unhinges me and I don't know where to begin,' he said, just managing to remain on the right side of charm. Although taken with them, he didn't want to make them think he was some kind of Lothario. The girls giggled together again, and he took this opportunity to slide the photograph out of his wallet and put it on the counter before them.

'I am seeking some information for a client. Have either of you ever seen this lovely lady?' The bolder of the two picked it up, examined the face pictured in it, and shook her head; then she handed it to her friend, who looked at the image for a little while and said 'no'.

'Well, she's lost and her husband is concerned about her,' observed Wilder. The girls asked him a few questions about who they were looking at, and where she came from, but he apologised to them.

'I'm sorry, there's a few details I have to keep quiet, but thanks for your help, ladies. I'm staying in the hotel in town, name of Huck Wilder; if you can think of anything, give me a shout.'

The store was getting busy by then so their attention was taken by actual paying customers. He walked around the store and showed the photo to a few of the other assistants, and then left by the main door. But just as he was walking along the road he heard a faint, breathless shout behind him. He turned and saw the smaller of the two shop assistants he had first seen. She had pink spots on her cheeks, more caused by accosting a stranger than the rush to get to him.

'Can I see that photograph again?' she asked. He obliged, and she scrutinized the girl's face for a few seconds.

'Maybe if you ask her brother he could help,' she said.

'What do you mean?'

'Well, we have a clerk working here who keeps the books, though today there's a bit of a fuss because he didn't turn up for work. If you took away that moustache and gave him long hair he'd be the double of that girl,' said the assistant.

'What's your name?' asked Huck.

'Em, short for Emmaline,' said the young lady.

'Well, you may have something there, Em,' said Huck. 'So where can I find this clerk of yours?'

'His name's Philo Babbington, and he's staying at the Brand place. They take in lodgers.' She gave him directions.

'I think you just cracked the code, lady,' Wilder reached for his wallet; he knew how much shop girls earned, and five dollars would be a huge tip for the young woman.

'I don't want your money, mister,' she said, and paused significantly, so that a slow smile drew across his face. He thrust out a hand that was almost as soft as hers, and they shook.

'Name's Huck, what time will I pick you up?'

'I finish at six, and I'll need to get changed. I'll meet you here at seven?'

'Sounds good to me! See you soon, little lady!' He tipped his hat to his date and strode off to his destiny.

EIGHT

HUNTED DOWN

Sheriff Palmer had returned to town the previous day. There was nothing else for him to do, but before his return he went to interview Birch and Carson at the lumber yard. Neither of them told him anything he didn't know, but he warned them that if they ever thought of lynching anybody on his watch again there would be serious consequences. They had both denied that that was what they were going to do, but he could see on their faces that they believed him.

Powell was a different matter; he had volunteered to ride into town with the sheriff, and annoyed Palmer by asking what was going to happen next.

'Far as I'm concerned I'm going to get one of my deputies to go with me, and we're going to track down Will and Philo.'

'When are you going to do this?' demanded Powell.

'What's it to you?' asked Palmer.

'Nothing,' said his companion as they rode into town. But as they parted company in front of the sheriff's office, Palmer thought to himself that it was far from nothing, judging from the expression on Powell's face.

Now that he was back in town the sheriff did something that was underrated in this world: he sat and thought about what he had to do. It was a big territory and he had a lot of work on his plate. Miners and cowboys were not the best behaved people, especially when they came into town – got roaring drunk and fought each other. He was overstretched and understaffed.

Somehow, in his heart, he knew that Will would be back, that this whole event was far from over. He had already asked his deputies to make regular patrols of the area and report back to him with any information, and he had asked Pete, Birch and Carson to do the same thing.

If Will returned to the area it would not be long before the information reached his ears, and he would not dare return to town. Palmer relaxed. He had time to put up his feet and just wait.

*

Rory Tunnock and Wesley Gandon went riding into the hills with their supplies. They had a tent and bedrolls, utensils, enough food for three days, and plenty of time.

'Where's he most likely to go?' asked Tunnock, who was not a deep thinker.

'Far as I'm concerned I know that Will James liked to stay in a guest house not that far from town, out towards

Grundy's trading post,' said Gandon, who was a great deal shrewder than his companion. 'I say that you and me, we stake out the Brand place, wait until he arrives back there, and take him down.'

'How would you know somethin' like that?' scoffed Tunnock.

'When the kid was with us he yapped somethin' awful,' said Gandon, 'and I guess I was the only one of us who really listened to him.'

'So we head out for the Brand place?'

'I guess so. Besides, there's an added attraction there for that bastard.'

'What's that?' asked Tunnock.

'There's a girl there called Betsy, one of the sweetest young things under the sun. Grundy was set on her... say...' Gandon was suddenly struck with an original thought, 'perhaps that was one of the reasons why Grundy's dead – James is after Betsy and old Sal was in his way.'

'Sounds as good a reason as any,' said Tunnock.

'Except, when you think of it, Sal was there when Josh bit the dust,' said Gandon, 'and that's kind of a better reason.'

They rode out to the Brand spread. It was not a sprawling estate, but the area around the guest house was overgrown because it had been somewhat neglected as land that could be farmed. This suited the new arrivals because it meant they could find a place where they could shelter without being seen.

They soon got off their mounts and set up camp fairly quickly. They were far enough away from the guest house that they could not be easily detected, yet they were close enough to be able to keep a look-out for their prey.

They ate some of their food and settled down for a short while. Both realized that this was a life they could live for a few days, retreating from all the troubles of the wider world. The fly in the ointment was that the situation could not last for long. They could live on bare rations and catch quail and rabbit a-plenty, but they both liked their home comforts, and it was the tail-end of summer. Autumn was coming in, and it had already rained on the way there.

'You know, I'm runnin' out of ready money,' said Gandon thoughtfully. 'I know we can get jobs and all that, but when we plug James we're goin' to be on the run for a while.'

'Not that long,' said Tunnock, 'and we'll get work real soon.'

'I get that, but the truth is that if we need to get out we'll need cash in hand.'

'What're you saying?'

'That new department store in town is making money hand over fist – what do you say that after we take care of Will, we go back to town and make our own finance?'

Tunnock thought about the matter. His landlady was tolerant, but even he could read the signs that she was going to throw him out soon. He had given her some rent in the last few weeks but it wasn't enough and she depended on the money. It meant that she would prob-ably bar him in the next few days. He, too, had seen that the store was making money hand over fist while he,

Tunnock, had gone all the way to Colorado and back without making a penny.

'All right,' he said, 'I'm in.'

*

Deek Powell did not know what to do. He was in a situation of his own making, he understood that, and he also knew what Will James was like. Will would never give up, he knew that, and after considering the matter for a while he decided that the best course of action was to beard the lion in his den. Powell had learned about the Brand ranch from the sheriff, and that James had fled with the other lodger. In his heart he knew that James had left to protect the other man, and he, too, thought that the lodger was going to return.

The only way to settle the matter was to go to the guest house and wait for the inevitable return of his nemesis. Which is why, barely an hour after the thought occurred to him, he was climbing the stairs to the porch and was knocking on the front door of the building. It was answered by a young woman who would have been attractive if it had not been for her red-rimmed eyes, and the hollows underneath them.

'Good mornin' ma'am. I've been thinkin' of doing some work around here, so I wondered if you had any rooms available.'

'I don't think we're taking in people just now,' said Betsy, for it was she.

'What's going?' asked a deep voice from behind her, and the old man shuffled into view.

'I was just telling this gentleman we're not taking anybody in,' said his daughter.

'Load'a rubbish,' said the old man. 'Come on son, you'll do just fine. How long ya stayin'?'

'But Pop, I thought we were going to give it a rest?' asked the girl.

'He's got money – you do, don't ya?' asked Old Brand.

'Yep, pay you up front for a coupla days,' said Powell.

'Good, real good, take the man's money…' said her father, '…make him a hot meal. Come on in son,' and her father stomped off to his own quarters, leaving the girl with a look of resentment on her pretty features. She stood aside and let the stranger enter.

'Sure could do with that a hot coffee,' he said, standing there in his riding clothes, holding his wide-brimmed hat by the rim.

'Go inside the dining area,' she said, 'I'll make you a coffee and get you some food; it's just eggs and bacon.'

'That'll do fine, ma'am,' he said.

'And you can take off your gun,' she said, 'no need for it indoors.' She held out her hand and waited as he reluctantly unstrapped his gun belt and handed it to her, bullets, gun and all. He had lied to the sheriff about only having a rifle. Luckily he hadn't been wearing the gun belt at the time. She carefully hung this inside a plain cupboard in the hall.

'I'll show you your room later. Now we can discuss payment.' He handed her ten dollars. It was most of what he had left, but he wasn't about to let her know this salient fact. The girl vanished, and later he was fed to his satisfaction.

She showed him his room, which was upstairs just beside the stairs. There was a great deal of resentment in the way she did this, and he guessed that she did not really want anyone in the building at the present time.

'I have to go now, Mr – sorry, I didn't ask your name.'

'Smith, John Smith,' said Deek figuring that if he broadcast his real name he might end up having to explain a few things to the sheriff if Betsy ever mentioned that he had been staying there.

She made his meal and brought it to him in the dining room.

'I hope you enjoy your stay, Mr Smith. I have to leave now. We're short on hands and I have to do some milking in the barn. In fact I'm a bit short on time altogether.' She hurried to the door and left.

Deek waited for a few minutes and went down to the hall, where he started to ease open the cupboard door.

'All right, young man?' asked a booming voice. Startled, he turned around and found that he was faced by the owner.

'Ah, Mr Brand,' he said. 'I thought I heard a noise, so I came downstairs.'

'See anything you like?' asked the old man. Deek snatched his hand away from the handle of the door.

'No, no, I'm fine.'

'Make sure that girl looks after you, she's been getting too big for her boots.'

'Betsy? She's a credit to you sir.'

'She's not bad,' and the old man, and stamped off towards the kitchen where he grumbled loudly about the need to make his own coffee. Deek sighed in relief, sneaked the door open, snatched his gun belt and made his way upstairs. The bed had a wrought-iron frame on which the flock mattress rested. He concealed his gun and belt underneath. He rested on top of the soft bed and tried to still his beating heart.

It was not the best situation, but he had a task now. He just had to wait and see to it that he called out Will James when the time came – and somehow, in his heart, he knew it would be soon.

*

Will was riding up the slope to the Brand house with the disguised girl beside him. It was early in the morning, the day after the two cowboys had decided to hide and wait for his arrival. When they heard the sound of horses clopping up the path it was the reason they scrambled out of their bedrolls – though the pair of them kept their heads down and did not dare breathe for about half a minute, as the animals passed so close to them they could have reached out of the undergrowth and touched them.

This might have seemed an ideal opportunity for them to launch their attack, but they were both in their long johns, having spent a cold, damp night in their hiding place, and they had wrapped up their weapons to keep them dry. If they scrabbled to get dressed and get their guns right at that moment, it would mean that they might bring attention to themselves, and the truth was that Gandon and Tunnock were united by one common factor: they were cowards, and did not want to take a chance. They both knew that Will James was ferociously well prepared, and even though they might take him down with an ambush, the operative word was 'might'. They both knew that if he got the slightest inkling that anyone was after him he would come after that person or persons, and neither of them wanted that to happen after what Will had done to Grundy.

So they let him pass, breathing once more when the two horses were gone. The two of them scrabbled into their clothes once the sound of the horses' hoofs had faded up the hill, then peered out of the undergrowth: they saw that Will and Philo were dismounting from their animals, with Philo going to the front door while Will led the animals round the side and to where the stables were located.

'Well, this sure is a tricky proposition,' said Tunnock. 'If we go near the ranch he'll come out and have a shootout with us.' The point was that neither of them wanted to be seen making their attack.

'Easy,' said Gandon, 'I've practised shootin' for years, I can knock a bottle off a fence at a hundred feet,' which incidentally was just about the distance they were away from the building. They both knew that this was about the greatest distance from which a handgun could be accurate when he was shooting, and he knew his barrel was worn, which also affected range. 'We just wait until he reappears, plug him and get outta here.'

'What about our gear?'

'Leave it, we just saddle up as fast as we can right now – you do it while I wait here. If you get it done real quick we'll get to do this together.' Grumbling under his breath, and cursing a little too, Tunnock went to where the horses were waiting in a copse further down. The animals had been fed nothing but grass and were not in the best of moods as he saddled them, but as he tightened the straps Tunnock hoped fervently that he was not going to miss the main event.

He came back and found that Gandon was still crouching on the damp grass with a look of concentration on his somewhat plain features. He twisted round as his companion arrived and looked discouraged.

'No sign of that bastard.'

They waited there for another ten minutes, which seems an eternity when you are crouching down in cold, damp undergrowth.

'Chrissakes, he must've gone in the back way,' said Tunnock, 'I'm goin' to get some grub.'

'Hell you will,' said Gandon, 'I've been here a lot longer than you. We'll both plug him when he comes out, but I get to eat first. Shout me when he appears and I'll come runnin'.' He vanished to get some food, leaving his uncomfortable companion where he was, before the other could argue. Using language that once more would have shocked his poor mama, Tunnock stayed where he was and kept looking out for the man who had caused them so much trouble.

*

When Betsy wearily answered the door, she wasn't expecting the sight that met her eyes.

'Philo, you're back,' she said, with a smile of pure pleasure, but which quickly melted away like the morning frost. 'You've had me so worried, I thought you would be dead in the wild country by now. Come in, hurry up.' She practically dragged her old companion into the building. A few minutes later they were joined by Will, who had come in through the back entrance after making sure that the horses were well stabled.

The patriarch of the ranch appeared as Will entered, and looked at him in silence for a few moments.

'So ya came back? I wouldn't advise ya to stay here for long, that sheriff's gunning for ya.'

'I won't need to stay for long,' said Will. 'Get Betsy and Philo, and follow me,' and he strode into the dining area where he had eaten so many of Betsy's plain meals while the others followed. Then Philo stepped away from the other three.

'I've decided to tell the truth,' said their former lodger. 'I think I owe you that much.' With one hand she reached up and – rather painfully – pulled off her moustache, and with the other lifted the tight cap off her head and shook her long hair down to her shoulders. The transformation could hardly have been more complete: before her hosts stood a good-looking and fairly tall young woman. The old man reeled back in astonishment, but Betsy gave the young woman a look of triumph.

'I knew it!' she said. 'That time when I held you, hugged you close before you went away, I could feel what you were.' The women went towards each other and embraced once more, but this time the tears flowed, to the discomfort of the two men.

'She's decided to go back,' said Will, 'but she's goin' to wait here until things get settled.'

'Will, I didn't say this while we were out on the trail,' said Pauline, who was once Philo, 'but those men who you suspect killed your brother aren't worth hunting down. Your brother's gone, he's never going to come back, and philosophically it makes no difference if you take your revenge or just leave. My name's Pauline, by the way.'

Standing there with Betsy – and the women had an arm around each other's waists like sisters with barely a year between them – the girl was looking at Will with shining eyes and slightly parted lips. She was truly beautiful, and for a moment he felt a stirring of something else than the bitter hatred that had been poisoning his mind for so long, distracting him from other instincts.

'Maybe you're right, Pauline,' said Will, the first admission that had passed his lips since he had heard of the disappearance of his brother. 'Maybe that's the way it should be, but you don't know these men like I do. I could just say it's all done, and go away, but that's not the way they work. You're clear Pauline, but I'm not, I wish to hell that was the case, but it just ain't the way things are going to turn out.'

'Come with me, we'll go to the sheriff, tell him the truth,' said the girl in a slightly desperate manner. 'He'll believe a great deal of what you have to say.'

'In the meantime I'll be on the wrong side of a cell door,' replied Will, 'I guess that now I'm his chief suspect, and I can assure you, young lady, that if there's one thing the law doesn't like it's a suspect running around who might do a lot more damage.'

'Like what?' challenged Pauline.

'Like gunning down witnesses or driving 'em off. No, I got to go out there again,' said Will, and he turned to Betsy and the old Brand. 'Will you two look after her?' he slapped down a fistful of dollars. 'That should take care of her for the foreseeable future.' He put a rough finger under Betsy's chin. 'I can see it trembling on your lips that you don't want my money, but I ain't buying you off, just paying a reasonable amount for a service. Now I'm getting my good old horse and I'm getting out of here.' He turned and gave a rueful smile to Pauline and turned back, only to see a shadowy figure in the doorway.

'Hey, Will!' said an unfamiliar voice. 'About time we met. Time to end all o' this.'

NINE

REVELATION AND TREACHERY

Palmer was a man who could rest easy. Even though he lived in a mining town through which there was a regular cattle drive and lone, sometimes crazed people who came through to look for their fortune in the hills, he was not easily stirred. He could quite easily eat a meal, go out a few minutes later, arrest a man and string him up, and then go back for dessert. He had done so in the past, but the Grundy murder – if it was murder – niggled at him in a way that most things didn't.

It was not just the fact that the trading post had been there most of his life, but the fact that he knew for certain that he was being lied to, and it wasn't by Will James. Many men have a reputation that spreads out from their actions in a place where more often than not the law is a matter of what is possible, but not always right or fair, and he knew that this was a man who, on losing his parents, had made sure that his brother was well taken care of. That kind of loyalty meant something in a world that was often cold and cruel.

In the middle of it all was the guest house. The Brand place, out of town and it should have been out of mind, but it was somewhere that Will James used when he wanted to rest in between jobs.

Palmer thought hard about what had happened with James. Here was a man who had stopped a lynching party from hanging a little clerk. By all rights he should have hung fire, allowed the sheriff to come in and examine the situation and put the little clerk away, possibly for his own safety, until he was exonerated. But Will James had fled with the man. It seemed to Palmer, thinking about Grundy and the vanishing of Josh James, that only one person could be responsible for the death of the trader.

That meant James had taken Philo away to protect him. The clerk was probably halfway to Colorado by now.

Then the sheriff reached the inevitable conclusion that once his clerk companion was well away, Will James would return and complete his task. It was for this reason that Palmer arose at an unearthly hour and went to the livery where he stabled his horse Oatus, fetched that animal from a sleepy livery keeper who blanched a little at seeing the plump man out at that time, mounted up and started making his way towards the guest house in the hills were this had all started.

He had waited long enough for the return of Will James. Even though he admired the man in his inner self, there was no denying the truth that James was now his chief suspect.

*

In their little kingdom in the trees and bushes, a good distance from the building, Tunnock and Gandon were waiting when Gandon dropped his bombshell.

'You know how you were off preparing some eats for us yesterday evening while I was on guard?'

'Yep,' said Tunnock tersely.

'I saw a new guest arrive at the Brand place, knock and get admitted.'

'So what? That's what they do, take people in. That Betsy, she's a beauty too, no wonder ol' Sal wanted to snap her up.'

'The new arrival was Deek Powell, and he was all soft and nice and 'yes ma'am, no ma'am, three bags full ma'am. Best of it is, he knows we're here, 'cos I met him and put the plan to him about what we were gonna do, even before I asked you.'

'Why the heck didn't you tell me?'

'I figured that being the kind of spineless low-down piece of piss that you are, as soon as you found out that little fact you would run out on our deal. Let Powell take care of our problem.'

'But that makes sense; we can get clean out of here without a stain against us.' Tunnock was already rising, but he was pulled down to his stealth position by a strong hand.

'You know what Deek's like; he messed up our chances in the mountains by killing that kid, and he's going to mess up here and now, but when he comes out of that there place we'll finish the job for him. I told him we'd be down here hidin', when it kicks off, if it's outside, we can help him.'

They waited with no more patience than before, Tunnock with a rising indignation in his heart.

*

'I guess you don't know much about me,' said Deek Powell, 'no one does, really, I knowed Sal from when I was a boy and it just about broke me when I saw him all dug up like that. That man was like a father to me.'

'Outside,' said Will, 'we'll do this like men.'

'Will James, when I faced up to you like that, I guess I wasn't expectin' anything else,' then Deek gave a grin that was such a travesty of the usual facial expression that for a moment Pauline and Betsy drew back in real terror. As the two men strode purposefully out of the building, Old Brand went to the hall cupboard, from which he drew out his faithful Winchester rifle. As Will moved, Pauline let a cry of despair fly from between her newly exposed, curved lips.

'Will, don't do this, he'll kill you.'

Will moved her to one side, but not roughly, rather with the regret of a strong man who is shifting a young child out of the way of thundering hoofs so that it doesn't get hurt.

'Wait here, out of the way,' he said. 'This is the end.'

He walked out of the building, following behind the man who had killed his brother.

This was an unexpected confrontation, and as the owner of the building came out to the porch holding his rifle, the two men turned and faced up to each other, guns at the ready in their low-slung belts. In each case the handles of the guns were turned outwards so that they could cross their arms, snatch them out and fire as quickly as possible. The front of the building had been cleared so there was a long stretch of low-lying grass, with a gravelled path just in front of the guest house. Their feet crunched downwards as they walked across this and on to the grass.

They still looked at each other, their eyes wide for any trace of treachery on either part. They were as tall as each other, but one man was weedy and sallow, and looked as if he might be blown over by a stiff breeze, while the other was as manly as they came, with his big, raw-boned frame, his firm stride, even firmer jaw, and the way he failed to flinch at the prospect of death, wearing his wide-brimmed hat to shade his eyes and let him focus more precisely on his actions.

'So,' said Will as they were taking up their positions, 'what was it, what did my brother do?' He could have added the words 'for you to end his life?' but he didn't, yet the phrase hung unspoken in the air between them. Powell was not, as might have been expected, defensive or defiant, instead he turned and looked at his opponent.

'Your brother, Josh, we started out an' he was all "let's do this" an' "let's do that", and then we got to the claim.

It was mine, my claim, an' what had happened...' his voice trailed off miserably, 'it was gone, jumped by the blackest-hearted sons-of-a-gun you ever met. Those bastards fought us off with Vulcans, an' had a minor fort dug in the hills. They were quite happy to kill the lot of us, so we returned empty, supplies runnin' out...' his voice trailed off again. 'That Josh, he just kept bitchin' and snortin' and bringing the lot of us to task. It all boiled over during the last food we had with us. Tunnock took more than he was entitled to, I always hated that weasel bastard, and we was coming to blows over it when Josh jumped in an' tried to get us to see some reason. We was both armed by then, an' he tried to calm it down, an' got in the way when I was going to shoot that pig's ass in the head. I was ill, too, we all were, he was the only one who wasn't – he was young, robust and in better health, didn't drink the water from the creek, y'see.' He looked at the implacable face of the older man who was slowly backing away from him. 'It wasn't meant, I was real sorry, I liked the boy.'

'You killed my brother, doesn't matter how or why, a young 'un snuffed out because of your stupid ambitions.'

'I guess that means you ain't about to forgive me, Will James?'

'You killed an innocent man, that's enough for me.'

While they had been speaking they had backed off from each other so they were at enough of a distance for the shoot-out to begin. Will had the front of the house beside him, but had backed up so much that he was close to the far side of the building. At the other angle, behind and to the side of Powell, were the trees and bushes that had been cut back from the property. It was obvious that they had to get down to the business in hand. Then all of a sudden Powell shouted: 'Get him, you pair of cowardly bastards!', and ducked away from the shoot-out that he had instigated. But Will James was not an idiot – he had seen what Powell was doing in backing towards the bushes, but just as he had with Grundy, he had not wanted to gun down a man in cold blood. Conversely he knew his way around treachery, and even before Powell had a chance to shout, Will was on the move. It might have been expected that since he was so near the side of the building he would have gone that way, but instead he gave an almighty roar and ran after the swiftly retreating form of the man who had pretended to face up to him.

There is no doubt that it is hard to hit a moving target, and more than that, Will had long legs and could cover a considerable amount of distance with each stride. As he ran there was the sound of pistols being discharged, and bullets flew past his swiftly moving body with an anxious whine from each like oversized insects, bullets that hit the side of the building. As James passed him, Old Brand gave a roar, raised his Winchester and fired towards the place where the shots were coming from. But he vanished from the porch as a pair of slim, but surprisingly strong hands gripped him from behind and pulled him back into the building. This was a wise move, because just a little while afterwards a couple of slugs thudded into the door in front of which he had been standing.

The truth was that Powell was a good runner, the building was on top of a high hill and he was running at ever greater speed down an increasing slope.

But then a bulky figure appeared on the lower slopes riding his horse, and tried to get in the way of the figure coming towards him, and snatched at his holster as he held the reins with his other hand, Powell fired his gun wildly and the shot just missed the sheriff, for it was he. Having to duck away from the blast so that it passed close to his head (it missed because Powell was still running, and it is just as hard to aim accurately when you are running as when you are aiming at a running man) the sheriff turned in the saddle and fired at Powell. It was more a matter of luck than judgement that he caught the man between the shoulders with one shot.

Powell gave a cry of pain, fear and rage and fell face downwards, quivered uncontrollably, and was still.

*

Will James was busy. The firing from the trees had stopped, but James was a man who owed his life to dealing with violent situations, and he sensed at once that those who had ambushed him were on their way out.

Firing with intent to murder does not endear the perpetrators of that act to those whom they have tried to kill. Will ran back the way he had come, sped around the side of the building and returned shortly on Shadow, his horse. He was riding bareback, because it had saved him time to put on just the bridle in one swift motion, and not the saddle. He spurred his horse on and Shadow cantered down the road, gathering speed, just as Gandon and Tunnock burst out of the undergrowth on their own steeds. These were quarter-horses, and good enough for everyday work, which was what they were usually used for – but they were not good enough to outpace a man who was not only an expert rider, but filled with what might be called righteous anger.

Will rode hard behind them, and despite having no saddle, soon began to catch up with them. Gandon, who was the bolder of the two, twisted around and took a pot shot at his pursuer. The bullet was one of those lucky ones that came perilously close, and Will felt a pain burn in his side as it whined past close enough to tear at his shirt. This was enough to infuriate him, and he spurred on Shadow once more – and this time he was so close to Gandon that he could not miss. He drew out his gun – holding the reins with the other hand – and shot Gandon in the shoulder. His horse made a whickering noise and reared in the air, throwing Gandon to the ground. This was not the only thing that happened. Tunnock, who was not far off, gradually brought his steed to a halt and held up his arms, hands waving in the air.

'Don't shoot, I surrender,' he snivelled.

'Get off,' ordered Will, 'and once you're down, keep your hands in the air.'

'Don't kill me, it was him,' said Tunnock, obeying the command and standing at the side of the track. He indicated Gandon, who was lying on the ground moaning because in falling off his steed he had broken a couple of bones in addition to the wound in his shoulder.

Will was going to leave him there – he wasn't going to go anywhere – and lead Tunnock up to the guest house at gunpoint so that he could put him into custody – but the sheriff arrived on his own mount, a large horse that was panting as it drew up beside the three men.

'Well, they're under arrest,' said the sheriff. 'I arrived and heard Powell shoutin' at you. I stayed amongst the trees lower down and I heard everything. He was a killer all right, and these two – well, that attack on you proves it all. He must've known that they were hidin' there, and he drew you out so that they could kill you.'

'I swear it was Wesley's idea. He must've been in league with Powell all the time and didn't tell me until were there, the sneaky bastard,' said Tunnock.

'Time to give up your bodies,' said the sheriff. 'Right, you can all surrender your guns and heave that sorry sack of shit across his horse; it's a good long ride into town, and the sooner we get there, the sooner this gets settled.'

'What do you mean "surrender your guns"?' asked Will. 'They were trying to kill me, the three of them. I'm the innocent party in this.'

'Will, put down your weapon, I don't want to have to shoot you,' said the sheriff. 'I've killed one man today, and that's enough. You're under arrest for the suspected murder of Sal Grundy.'

TEN

WOMEN ON A MISSION

Huck Wilder was not exactly cursing his fate. He had been with the young lady who had met him after the department store closed. Emmaline had proven to be a very forthright and compliant young lady. He had taken her to a respectable dining establishment, where they had partaken of a meal. Then he had taken her for a ride in his horse and buggy into the hills, where she had allowed him to make love to her for a most satisfactory period of time.

During the meal he had questioned her about Philo, amongst others, making it look as though he was just talking about her work in general. But the things he learned about the little clerk had given him a growing conviction of what he was dealing with. People saw things just as they wanted, and if someone said they were a man – even one as weedy and quite frankly as unconvincing as Philo seemed to have been – they believed that story because it was what they were told.

In his own life, as a man who fixed things, he had noticed that a cheery smile and a good suit were enough to convince people that he was a businessman, and those two things had made him a good living over time.

He had left Emmaline late, because of course he had to take her back to the family home, so he had not got back to his lodgings until nearly midnight, and he had partaken of a few drinks while he was there. So it was that he slept until nearly ten, and awoke with a head that not only ached, but reacted to the slightest noise and smell. By the time he forced himself to eat a large fried breakfast and drank four cups of coffee he felt better, but time was getting on and he had a job to do.

He was walking out of his lodgings to go and fetch his horse from the livery when, like many others, he saw a strange procession come into town. Will James and Rory Tunnock were leading their horses, while a third one was following obediently after with a wounded man on its back. The sheriff had a gun trained on the two men. Palmer did not waste any time, but shouted out to one of his deputies, who ushered the two men into jail, while Gandon was taken away for the local sawbones to patch him up. Gandon was not saying anything because he was unconscious or dead.

Wilder stood and watched these events, fascinated by them just as many of the other locals were, but he could not see any way in which they were connected with his mission. He finally fetched his horse and, still a little the worse for wear, made his way to the Brand spread.

Many thoughts went through his head as he took his time on the journey, and they were mainly to do with how he would plan his operation. If Philo, who was really Pauline, was there, it would not do to attack her straightaway – there would be witnesses to begin with, and he couldn't have that. No, he would pretend to be a prospective guest who wanted to pause in his commercial travelling and stay at the guest house because it was a pleasing place in which to live for a few days before he had to go back to work.

He would find out if she liked to spend any time alone, anywhere, then he would be there waiting for her, and once she appeared he would do what was necessary and make sure that he was able to collect his reward. Then there would be a much greater reward to follow.

He winced as his head crashed a little at the intensity of so much thinking after a celebratory night on the booze. That was another detail – he would have to make sure that the night before the deed he had an early bed and was well rested. They say that the early bird catches the worm – well, getting up early was going to catch him a little bird and make his fortune.

Once the deed was done he would go back and make love to young Emmaline before ditching her, too, and riding off to inform Walker that he was now the proud owner of a large ranch and that no one could take it off him.

Walker had asked Wilder to inform him first where his wife was, and had then taken off in the direction of Riverton. Wilder knew the distance was vast and time-consuming; the girl might not even be there on his return

117

if Wilder spoke to Walker before taking any action. He made the decision to carry out the deed on his own.

On his way to the ranch two horses passed him, going at a pace that made his look as if it were practically at a standstill. Each was ridden by a slim figure wearing the kind of clothes he did not associate with women – black trousers, boots and coats, and they had wide hats pulled down low over their heads, while their mouths were covered with bandannas – but he could still tell they were women as they passed him, women who looked as if they were on a mission.

*

Will was in his cell, alone. The other two prisoners were in another cell nearer the back of the prison. The doctor had mended Gandon as best he could, digging the bullet out of his shoulder and splinting his broken arm. There was nothing he could do about the broken nose, it would just have to mend on its own, but he had given the prisoner a good dose of laudanum, then the deputy had hauled him off to jail and landed him on the wooden bench in the cell that served as possibly the hardest bed known to man. He had a flock pillow and a grey blanket for comfort, and that was about all.

Will stood up and put his hands on the bars. He looked straight at Palmer, who was sitting at a robust deal desk, which it was rumoured had saved his life when he ducked beneath it after a cowboy, bent on revenge, had thundered into his office and tried to shoot him.

118

'I guess you did the right thing sheriff, but I need to talk to you in private.'

Palmer was chewing a leg of a chicken that had been kindly roasted for him by the widow along the road who had her eye on him. He gulped and swallowed before answering with a shake of the head.

'Tell your story to the circuit judge, Will – looks to me as if all this worked out real good. My deputies have gone off and fetched your friend Powell, he'll soon be decorating a slab at the undertakers.'

'You don't understand, there were circumstances.'

'You're a murderer,' screamed Tunnock from the other cell. 'You deserve to hang.'

Will did not even look round at the other man. He backed away from the bars and sat down on the cot in his cell and looked at his captor. He shrugged his shoulders, lay down and tipped his hat over his face. He was not a man to rail against the vagaries of fate, and he was well known in the district, so there was a good chance that the jury – twelve men tried and true – would believe his tale. On the other hand, he might get them on a bad day; if so he would be swinging from a noose in front of an appreciative crowd faster than you could order a beer in The Brass Keys.

Palmer got up, having finished his chicken leg, bones in his hand, and went to the door of his domain. He was a tidy man, quite fussy in a lot of ways, and didn't want debris in his office, so he threw away the bones up the road. Just as he was doing this two riders thundered to a halt and drew up outside the building. They had an air of urgency about them, particularly in the way they yelled the words 'Sheriff!' and 'We want to see you!', which alerted him to this fact.

The two women pulled the bandannas off their faces and stared at the fat lawman. Betsy did not waste time.

'Sheriff, you've got to listen to us. Will is not a murderer.'

'I was with him,' said Pauline. The sheriff looked at her. 'Who are you?' he asked doubtfully, and then he peered at her a little more closely. 'You're the puny clerk Philo!' This might have seemed a reason for him to reject an audience with them, but in fact it made him pay them more attention. 'All right, I gotta tell you, that sun's hot and I've just eaten. I'll give you five minutes.' He looked at her steadily, still thinking he was looking at an undersized male. 'Guess I should pull you in as the suspect for the Grundy killin'. But you came here on your own and there's somethin' about you...' his voice trailed off. 'I'm giving you the benefit of the doubt, seems to me some of these ones here had more reason to kill him.' He stared at her again and she wondered if he suspected what she really was.

Pauline stood there and explained about the attempted lynching, and the fact that Will had saved her life, and had put himself at considerable risk to see that she was safe. Betsy added that when Powell admitted that it was he who had killed Josh, Will was still willing to give him a chance and engage in a fair fight.

'You could make just as much of a case against me,' said Pauline. 'I was out that morning and I came back after Grundy was dead, but here I am.'

'You know what, that might not be a bad idea,' said the sheriff. 'Guess I could find room for you in there. The county ain't too fussy about who shares a cell with whom, and it won't be the first time I've locked up a woman. Usually for cat fighting, so it would make a change to take a sober one.' Instead, he turned his back on the two women and a minute later shouted them into the building. He led them into an annexe next door to the jail. It was not exactly home from home, being a room with a cot much like that used for the prisoners in their cells, shoved in the corner.

'Sometimes a man can't get home,' said Palmer, 'if it's been a busy night, so this is where we rest.'

'I don't understand…' began Pauline, but she was talking to a retreating back. The reason was revealed a moment later when a puzzled-looking Will came in, shackled, with a gun pointed at his back. He had not seen them coming in because he had been lying in his cell at the bottom of the building with his hat over his eyes when they entered. He looked astonished to see the two women there.

'Now,' said the sheriff, moving so that all three of them were lined up and facing him. 'I've listened to these young women saying what a good guy you are. How's about you tell me what really happened that day at Grundy's trading post?' This was a crucial moment in their relationship with Palmer. He was asking Will to make a confession, and this is not always a good thing to do, because the words of those making the confession can be twisted in front of a jury.

121

'The truth is, *he* attacked *me*,' said Will. 'I came to see him in good faith because he knew something about what had happened to my brother.' He stopped, and for the first time since he had been arrested his face worked with emotion. 'That boy, he was all I had left in the world, but he was trusting and liked people. I set him up with a real good job with Oregon Pete, making wheels and repairing carriages, steady work, and he was good with his hands. Now he's dead, all because he decided to try and get rich quick on a claim that fooled all four of 'em.'

'But what happened with Grundy?' asked the sheriff.

'When I came back from my latest job in Arizona I heard about Josh, in town, that he had vanished, feared murdered, so I went real early to speak to Grundy. His heart was full of fear, and instead of talking he fired at me, the worst thing that can happen. I didn't have time to run so I fired back in self-defence. Yes, sheriff, I killed him, but he would have killed me.'

'Sheriff Palmer, I have something to tell you,' said Pauline, who had introduced herself to him by her real name a moment before. 'It's the truth. I went out early that morning before Betsy was even out of her bed, and she's a real early riser. She just assumed that I was out at my usual time because I came *back* at my usual time.'

'What're you trying to say, young lady?' asked Palmer.

'I had ample time to get to the trading post, and the truth is, I was there because *I* was going to kill Grundy. I saw what he did to the woman who had become my best friend. The thing is, I *saw* the fight between Will and Grundy, and it's exactly as Will said. He was just asking a few questions, Sal panicked, thought he was being blamed for something he hadn't done, and attacked Will. He fired quite a few shots, Will tried to escape, but when one went into the store right beside his head Will had to retaliate, so he did, and he was as shocked by what had happened as anyone.'

'How come he didn't notice you?'

'It was a twilight time of day, crepuscular you could call it, and a little misty, too, and I was at a corner of the trading post wearing dark clothes, and both of them were otherwise engaged as you might say. I slipped off really quickly while Will was deciding what to do, rode back to the guest house as fast as I could and laid low.'

'You must've got a helluva shock when I turned up with a lynch mob,' said Will ironically. Despite the situation he and the girl exchanged the briefest of smiles.

'I thought I was dead,' she said, 'but the situation I was in made me want to keep hiding for as long as possible, and this man risked everything to save a young clerk he didn't even know.'

'So why didn't you come to *me* like you should have?' asked Palmer.

'Because I wanted to get the man who had killed my brother,' said Will, 'once that was done I would have come to you and surrendered.' Normally this would have seemed like a laughable thing to say, but from the tall, weathered cowboy it seemed like a simple statement of truth. 'I guess I've made the bed of all beds, and it comes down to a jury,' he said.

'Wait, sheriff, you have to let him go, it was self-defence,' said Betsy. The two women looked at him with wide eyes.

'Well, I guess this territory has a kind of unwritten law,' said the sheriff, 'that if a man wants to preserve his life and he's being shot at, then his attacker can expect what's going to happen to him.' He gave the three of them a severe look. 'And it comes down to what a jury decides.'

'Put me back in the cell,' said Will wearily. He began to shuffle towards the door.

'Wait, did I tell you to move?' barked Palmer. Will froze – it was obvious that he could expect no mercy from that direction. But Palmer took the keys from his belt with one hand, holstered the gun with the other, picked the correct key and unlocked the shackles from the legs of his prisoner. They clattered to the floor.

'I saw the bullet holes in the wall at Grundy's,' said Palmer, 'an' they were recent. Besides that, I heard the way Powell shouted at them to kill you, and I knew that your brother was gone, presumed dead. I know you of old, the way you've been, an' I believe you.'

'But what is the county going to say?' asked Will.

'When it comes to matters like this,' said the sheriff, 'I *am* the county! Now get the hell out of here before I change my mind.'

ELEVEN

DENOUEMENT!

Huck Wilder was the kind of person who seemed to strike it lucky. He had been lucky when it came to the identification of the missing girl, now he was in front of a garrulous old man who wanted to get a great deal off his chest.

'Howdy stranger,' said the old man, 'come looking for a room for a few nights have ya? Or are ya from the sheriff's office? Just to let you know, the body's been taken away, the two deputies just came, hauled him away on the back of a cart.'

'What body?' the new visitor was genuinely baffled. 'What's been going on here, mister?' The old man seemed to shake himself like a dog that had just come out of a river.

'Sorry, don't mean a thing to you, an' it won't affect your stay.'

'Well, do you have a room here?'

'Sure have, comfy too, and the daughter'll see you're fed right. Come right in, mister.'

'Just a couple of things to ask – is it busy right now, your guest house?'

'Not now it ain't – one of our so-called guests, well he bought a lot of trouble just a short whiles back,' said Brand, 'so we got just one now, a young lady, not bad looking either.' It was obvious that he could have said more, but he buttoned his lip.

'Oh, what does she like doing?'

'Keeps real quiet, likes to go for a morning ride, 'bout seven in the morning, just about the time we rise. She was with us before, but kinda different. In the evenin' she likes to read in her room, expect she'll do the same as before.'

'Well, that's fine,' said Wilder, 'sorry to hear you've had trouble. Here's a deposit,' he gave the old rancher twenty dollars. 'My name's Smith, John Smith, I've got to go back into town, I've got business there, I do commercial travelling. I'll be back some time this evening unless I have to stay over in town for business reasons. So where does this young lady like to go on her rides?'

'Oh, just down the main trail towards the trading post,' said Brand.

'Oh well, perhaps we'll all have a drink together tomorrow night,' said Huck. He tipped his hat to his supposed host, mounted his horse and rode off. He took an alternative route back into town where there was little chance of meeting anyone, so that as few people as possible would see his face.

He had no intention of coming back, at least not until very early in the morning.

*

Betsy was up early as usual. Even Will, who was no slouch in that department, was still sound asleep in his room. Her father had been in an unusually good mood the previous night, despite the impending loss of his guests. In addition Betsy had a lot of work to do because her father had neglected his chores as usual and she had to milk the cows – luckily they had only three – feed the pigs and the hens, and make sure the crops were watered. Pauline, seeing what she was up against, had given her a hand so the girl was finished much earlier than she otherwise would have been.

Pauline had got together with Will afterwards. He had done his part by grooming and feeding the horses and making sure they were well rested for what was going to be a long journey. She found him in the stables looking after Shadow.

'I guess I didn't thank you enough for what you did,' he said.

'I guess you didn't,' she replied.

'Were you really there?' he asked. 'I never saw you.'

'I wouldn't lie, even for you,' she answered. 'I saw it all, and you know, I'm glad, because I really was going to blow out his miserable brains.'

'So where do we go from here?'

'I guess I'll do what you said, and go back, confront that horrible man who married me for my property and not my personal qualities.'

'You certainly have a few of those,' he said, which coming from him was a compliment. 'I'm coming with you, of course,' he said.

'I thought you were going to say that, but I guess I'm the one in trouble and I should finally face up to my responsibilities.'

'You need me,' he said. 'What if he cuts up rough?'

'I thought that violence was wrong,' said the girl, 'and when he treated me the way he did, something inside me just crumbled, and I ran because I had lost everything in the world that was dear to me, especially my father. In that kind of sorrow, the man you've married is supposed to love and look after you, and instead he tried to destroy me. I still think violence is wrong, but I'm going back to tell him we're getting divorced and there's nothing he can do about it.' She tilted her chin and looked at him with determination written in her eyes. 'I know this could end badly – very badly – but I tried running away, and it didn't work. I would rather face up to the world than skulk around like this any longer. I've reached a limit, and now I… I have something to live for.'

'I don't want him to cut up rough with you again,' said Will.

'I have a man who runs the ranch, John Burrows. I think I did the worst thing possible; I left the ranch in his hands and a note telling him I was running away, but not where.'

'You're still not fit; you need me by your side.' The girl looked at him, stepped forwards and put a slim hand on his strong forearm, bare because grooming horses was hot work and he had rolled up his sleeves.

'I've never thanked you properly, really.' His head was turned towards her and he was leaning down a little to address her fully. Caught in the moment he turned fully towards her, their faces so close she could catch the manly scent that came off him, and he could feel her soft breath on him – and then their lips met in a long, passionate kiss that neither wanted to end, and he wrapped her soft body in a strong embrace, and she felt cared for like never before.

When they finally stopped, he stepped back looking a little dazed, both at his actions and his reaction to her. The young woman, on the other hand, did not look troubled at all. She had an air of satisfaction about her that he could not put his finger on, making her more assured than she had ever been.

'As I was saying, I have to do this on my own,' she said. 'You, you mean more than anything to me Will, but I have to make this right.'

'And after that?' he looked incredulous. 'I know that I have to protect you, it's as simple as that.'

'I've changed,' said the girl. 'You've changed me, and all of this too, so I have to go.'

'We're returning together, and that's it!' he said. After they had discovered each other, it was the right path to take, and the girl's face suddenly hardened.

'I love you; damn you Will James, but never again will anyone tell me what to do!' He came towards her, but she held up an imperious hand: 'Don't!' and then swept away from him and out of the stable. For a moment he stood there, muscles showing in his arms as he bunched his fists, his jaw thrusting forwards while his feet took a similar path, but then he stopped short. He had been a married man, and he knew that the worst way to deal with a woman is to chase after her and continue with the argument. He shook his head and returned to grooming the horses.

*

Pauline set out on her early morning ride with a set look on her face; she had been amiable and polite with Will during their evening meal of pork, potatoes and beans, but she had not discussed moving on, and he had been wary, almost polite in return, although being a little rough and ready, along with his naturally taciturn disposition, had made polite conversation problematic.

She had always liked to go out riding on her own in the early hours because it was a time of day when the world was coming alive – even as Philo, working long hours in the department store, she had kept up the habit. She went out for about forty minutes, and this seemed to clear her mind for the day ahead. She was wearing her green slicker, the one with the hood, and that was good because it was raining, a faint drizzle that came down lightly but steadily, but not heavy enough to spoil her enjoyment of the ride.

She was too busy with her thoughts to notice the rain. It was as if in the last few days her mind had emerged from a fog. She knew a big part of it was the loss of her father, and the fact that in that loss she had turned to the man who had sworn to love and protect her, only to find out that he wanted the estate and not her. The shock, combined with the grief, had nearly driven her out of her mind, had stopped her from being the eternally strong woman she had been for her father. It was the reason why she had run away, hiding from her troubles, dressing as Philo.

She knew that Walker could not inherit the estate until she was dead, and she also knew that she never wanted to have him as part of her life again – but mostly she just wanted the space to mourn not only the death of her father, but the untimely demise of her marital relationship with the man she thought she had loved. In a way, her disappearance had been a form of revenge against Walker.

The rain became heavier as she went down the trail. She was not so much concerned for herself, but for her horse, so she decided it was time to go back. She knew one thing, if she wanted to face Walker she wanted to do it alone, and not risk the life of the man she loved. She set her jaw, and resolved she would face her husband and tell him she wanted the divorce he so richly deserved.

It was then that she became aware of another horseman coming towards her on the trail. It was still early in the morning and she rarely met anyone on her outings. Normally such riders were going somewhere, and quickly too, so she would exchange a brief nod with them and continue on her way. But this horseman had his hat pushed down low on his head, and as he came closer he lifted his arm and with one stroke of a stout stick hit her sideways with a sweeping blow that swept her off her steed and to the ground.

Her horse reared, whickered, and pounded off down the road. The man brought his own steed to a halt beside the form on the ground. She was winded, unhurt except for a few bruises, but he got off his horse, grabbed her by the neck and pulled her to the side of the trail.

'Got to make this look like a robbery,' he said, starting to pull up her slicker, 'it's a little wet, but no reason why I can't have a bit of fun in the process.' She began to protest, but he smacked her across the face, and although not tall, he was solidly built, and she was still trying to catch her breath. His weight bore down on her, and she was helpless.

*

Will was an early riser, but he was not early enough. He got up that morning, saw to his simple toilet, and met Betsy on the way downstairs.

'Is Pauline up?' he asked.

'She's gone,' said Betsy.

'What do you mean, "gone"?'

'Steady yourself cowboy, she's just gone out for a morning ride, like she always does. She did it even when she was Philo. Did you really think she was going to go away without saying goodbye?' She put a hand on his muscular forearm. 'I know you want to protect her, but she's going to see this through.'

Will, though, was not as trusting as he might have been. He didn't say anything, but went out the back of the building to the stables, saddled up and went after her. Being a trail rider he was used to seeing the signs of where a horse had passed, and as soon as he went out the front of the building he could see that she had taken her usual route.

Prudence then entered his soul and he thought of returning to the guest house, but then he experienced a sense of rebelliousness that coursed through him like a tide. He was just as entitled to a morning ride as the woman he loved, and if their paths coincided, then so be it. Besides, there was something bracing about the morning air he told himself as he rode onwards, studiously ignoring the drizzle that bounced off his wide-brimmed leather hat, while Shadow, being a horse, wasn't bothered by the light rain at all.

It was an absurd situation, but he thought that if he could speak to her in the open she would change her mind and accept his support.

He was riding along the trail now that led to the ill-fated trading post where all of this had started. The air was cool and refreshing, and he knew that this was the life for him whatever else happened in the world.

A riderless horse came towards him, moving slowly now, and there was another horse standing patiently without a rider further down the track. Will was the kind of person who knew one horse from another at a glance, and he should know this one because he had groomed it just the day before. He gritted his teeth, dug in his spurs and his steed galloped down the track towards the other horse that was standing there patiently awaiting the return of its owner. The damp ground absorbed the sound of the animal's hoofs, and it was not long before he was at his target. He barely waited for Shadow to come to a halt before he was off the back of the animal.

What he saw at the side of the road horrified him: it was another man of lesser height but solidly built, and he was attacking Pauline in a way that made it clear exactly what his intentions were. Pauline, it seemed, was semi-conscious, and the man had some kind of cudgel at his side.

Will gave a curse that he used only in extreme circumstances, ran forwards and grabbed the man by the collar, and with a strength that seemed much more extreme than normal, heaved him away from the girl and on to the path. Pauline gave a startled groan and tried to move, but fell back.

The stranger was not about to give up easily, and he was strongly built. He heaved himself to his feet, the slick blue garment around him glistening with wetness from the undergrowth, and crouched in front of his assailant.

Will badly wanted to go and see how Pauline was, but he was in real danger: he had set out without his gun belt because he had left in some haste, so he was unarmed. He had nothing but his naked fists with which to fight. Knowing this, but also knowing that attack is the best form of defence, he gave a roar and leapt at the stranger.

The man threw off his slicker, pushing it into Will's face and fell away. It was obvious that he did not really want to fight, and was heading for his horse. Will fell back and saw that the stranger was armed, a Colt 45 at his side. Once he was on his horse the attacker would shoot both him and Pauline, because he could not let them get out of this situation alive.

Will threw the garment to one side, ran forward and snatched at the back of the stranger, managing to get hold of his shirt and pulling him away from the horse. This unbalanced Pauline's attacker and he had no choice but to turn – but as he did so he snatched the gun from his holster.

Even by the way the man held the gun Will could tell that he was not experienced at using such a weapon, and the safety catch was on. This was the undoing of the stranger as far as the gun was concerned, because Will, instead of trying to snatch it from him, gave a desperate kick that sent the weapon spinning out of the stranger's hand.

At this point Will was tempted to allow the man to get on his horse and ride away, but this was not something that could happen. Who knew the stranger? Why was he attacking Pauline? It was obvious that this had been planned and was not some random event.

'You had to poke your nose into something that's none of your business,' said the attacker. 'I guess it's just you and me, stranger.' As he said this, he was circling round, obviously calculating his chances of getting his gun back.

Will said nothing, but bunched his fists and attacked. He had been in his share of bar fights and knew how to punch out an opponent. But the man he was fighting had obviously boxed before: he tucked in his elbows, lowered his chin, bunched his fists and readied himself for the attack.

The two of them slugged it out on that pathway, their horses standing nearby, and from the start they were equally matched. Although Will was bigger, his more compact opponent could move more quickly, and he had a fast uppercut that connected more than once with Will's chin. His second blow was so hard that it almost knocked Will off balance. He knew he could not fall, or the attacker would be on him with his boots along with his fists. Will was able to counter with several blows to the body when the stranger let his guard down to punch at his opponent. His blows were hard and unrelenting, and the stranger groaned aloud. He circled again and Will punched him hard on the chin. The stranger fell, but as he rose, scrambling back on the wet path he was holding the mud-spattered gun that he had managed to recover from the ground. His eyes were glinting in the gathering daylight, and it was obvious that he had released the safety catch on his weapon. It looked as if Will was about to get a hole blasted in his body, and he was not going to get any mercy, he could see that from the expression his attacker's face.

Then a figure loomed out of the undergrowth holding a stout stick in her hand, and that stick descended not once, but two, three, four times on the head of the man who was attacking Will. The man gave a groan, fell to his knees and pitched forwards on to his face. The girl dropped the stick, a glazed expression on her face and stumbled forwards into the arms of the man she loved.

TWELVE

DAY OF RECKONING

Back at the guest house Huck Wilder, who had been brought there like a sack of potatoes on the back of his own horse, opened his eyes and groaned loudly.

He was lying on the porch of the very guest house he had visited the day before. The wooden boards were hard against his back and there was a wide, elderly face staring down into his. Wilder had a wound on his head, but he could feel it had been dressed with a linen bandage. It still hurt like hell.

'Yep, he's with us,' said Betsy's father. 'Don't know why ya bothered keeping him alive. Ya shoot rabid dogs in the head and bury them out the back. Just say the word and I'll deal with him,' and as he said the words he shook his trusty Winchester in front of the man's eyes. Startled, Wilder tried to get to his feet and found that his arms were bound at his side.

Betsy, Will and Pauline all loomed into view and stared down at him one by one, the last person with a look of such hatred that he felt his insides churn. Then, worse torture in a way, they all vanished out of his view and began to talk about him.

'I reckon we get rid of him,' said Will.

'Yep, I'll do it,' said the older man, 'make it clean, on the grass, jest drag him down the steps, bullet in the head, bury the crittar in the bushes.'

'That sounds about right to me,' said Will calmly.

'He deserves nothing less,' said Pauline.

'Wait, wait,' yelled out Wilder frantically, his voice hoarse with panic. Like many men who were prepared to attack a defenceless woman, he was at heart a craven coward who would crumble at the first sign of real trouble. His fight with Will had been mostly caused by the fact that he was trying to run away, and didn't want his evil deeds to be discovered.

'What do you want, dog?' asked Will, coming over and looming over the wounded man.

'Let me...help me...I'll talk, listen, it wasn't me, not really.'

'You're goin' to tell me a big boy did it an' ran away?' asked Will. There might have been a trace of sarcasm in his tone. However, he relented, and with the help of Brand, pulled the solid captive over to the panelled wall and sat him up with his hands still bound, so that Wilder was looking outwards over the main road that led to the building. Will and Brand stood in front of him, the older man holding his rifle in a way that indicated he was ready to spring into action at a word from the younger man.

'I need water,' croaked Wilder. Brand fetched the kind of canteen used by riders on a long journey, uncorked it and put it to the lips of their involuntary visitor. Wilder drank deeply and long. 'Thanks,' he said.

'Ain't for your comfort,' said Will, 'might be the last drink you ever get. Deliver, stranger.'

'I'm a man for hire,' said Wilder, 'I was hired by Troy Walker.' When he said the name there was a cry of outrage from one of the nearby women, and he knew which one. 'He asked me to make sure his wife wouldn't bother him again.' He seemed to realize what was happening. 'I wasn't going to kill her, honest, I was just going to make sure that she knew, and tell her that he had warned her well off, and that now she had vanished she was to stay vanished. I wasn't going to kill her, honest.'

'Liar,' said Pauline, coming into view and standing over him and stamping one of her shapely feet. 'You were going to rape me and strangle me, you bastard. Give me that rifle, I'm ending this now.'

'Aww, don't fire that bullet through him now!' declared the old man. 'You're gonna mess up the side of the building, an' it was jest painted a short whiles ago!'

'Look, don't kill me,' said Wilder with true terror. 'I'll tell you everything...' and he did, from his first meeting with Walker, which was before Troy had married Pauline. 'He told me that he knew about old Ryder, who was failing and that his daughter was easy pickings. He would marry her, and then when she inherited it all he would get it all off her, and it would be real easy to dispose of her...' He realized what he had just admitted, and added '...not that I was goin' to do that, I was just going to warn her off real good.'

'Give it to me,' said Will, and he was not talking to their prisoner. A moment later he waved a quill pen, ready dipped, and a sheet of paper in front of the man. 'Pauline here, she's a real quick and ready writer, she's been workin' as a clerk for months and she wrote down every word you said just fine and dandy on a sheet o' vellum. Son, I'm going to untie one of your hands, the one you write with, an' you're going to sign this.'

'No,' said Wilder, 'I can't!'

'It's your choice,' said Will. 'This way you get to live longer, the other, I just leave it up to my friend here, and he's got a hankering to see how good his ol' Winchester works at a close range. Your choice...' Wilder was sobbing by now, but just gave a brief nod of his head. 'You right-handed?' asked Will – another nod. Wilder's hand was untied, the quill put into his free hand, and he signed the document against the same tray on which Pauline had been writing. Will handed the confession to Betsy, who waved it around gently to dry the ink while Will retied his prisoner.

'We'll get you to the sheriff some time,' he said. 'He'll make sure you get a fair trial, which is better than what you were goin' to do with this young lady.' They all departed, leaving Wilder tied up against the wall, sobbing, knowing that his riches would never appear. He had lost his chance of blackmail forever.

Will and Pauline rode towards Riverton. They were not speaking much, but as the land changed Will could sense that Pauline was taking her journey hard, her shoulders stooping and her horse slowing when they came to the boundary of the two thousand acres that belonged to the Ryder family. She was dressed as Philo for the last time, and looked every inch the clerk, with her white, stiff-collared shirt, string tie, black jacket and loose trousers. She played the part so well that he could understand why she had been able to fool her companions in the store for three months.

'Penny for them,' he said, wondering what was wrong, given that they had already discussed the matter.

'He was my husband,' she said, 'I did love him once, this is so final.' Will knew that women were creatures with deeper feelings than men, and a lot more complex, but it didn't mean he could really understand them.

'This man wanted you dead, young lady, still does, really. He's gonna get a helluva shock.'

'He was so handsome and charming,' she said, with what he suspected was a trace of a sniffle in her voice. 'How could he do these horrible things to me?'

'Some men, they have all the words in the world,' said Will, trying to articulate something that he felt deeply, 'and they make people feel the way they want 'em to feel. But what they are is shallow, like a beautiful stream, you want to bathe in it when it's a hot day, an' the surface looks all cool an' inviting, but when you try and bathe it don't work, you just splash around up to your ankles but there's really nothin' there.' He realized that she was looking at him with wide eyes.

'Will, your summation of his character is straightforward and true.' She straightened up in the saddle and they rode onwards together, her back stiffening with resolve.

The Ryder spread was one of the bigger ranches in the territory, and once the two of them opened one of the wooden gates and rode on to her land he was not surprised to see the large numbers of cattle that wandered around. Knowing how much his new love had inherited, and actually seeing the extent of her property, were two different things. He could see not just the cattle, but several feed sheds and barns, and as they drew nearer to the main building, even a general store, of a kind, all on her land.

'That's run by Zachariah Jones,' she said. 'He used to ride the trails for dad, and when he retired he offered to open a store on the land here, where people could get their supplies instead of having to ride for miles into town on either side.'

'This place is more like a small village,' he said. 'You've got buildings over there where the workers stay, not bunkhouses, but proper clapboard houses.'

'Well, they have families, some of them,' she said. 'We do have one or two bunkhouses further out, and one or two along the trail.'

Her home, when they came towards it, was in the very centre of the ranch complex. It was a large building three storeys high, which had been added to over the years. She was able to explain the size of the building quite easily.

'I had brothers, cousins, and lots of other relatives. Dad was real hospitable when I was a kid, and well before I was born – I was a late child. He used to have people over here all the time, and he held jamborees for the workers, too. He believed in hard work, but he believed in play, and he played hard. It was only when he got older and his health declined that he turned more reclusive.'

'I still don't understand why you ran away from all of this,' said Will. 'Surely you had friends amongst the women here who could help you?' Her back stiffened again and she looked at him with a slight trace of scorn.

'You really don't understand, Will. I had made a huge song and dance about my wonderful husband, what a marvellous man he was – but then within weeks, after the death of Dad, it had all crumbled.'

'Yep, I can see that,' said Will unexpectedly. 'You had pinned all your hopes an' dreams on a man who would be with you through all the ups an' downs in life, and he just turned out to be plain bad. You must've felt you were demeaned and that no one would believe you – and that might've been the case,' he screwed up his face. 'I hate this thing they call "charm" – the ones who have it, let's face it, they're wordsmiths, they carve little empires out of thin air, and at the end of the day they're nothing.' He said these words with such passion that she knew she had touched a real, raw nerve, and for the first time she gave him a look of real compassion.

'Your wife,' she said, 'what was she like?'

'She ran off with one of your glib guys,' said Will, 'went to Chicago and the big lights and all o' his empty promises, divorced me. She's dead now; someone got word to me that died of a fever, a real common thing – so end of story.'

So far their presence on the ranch had not been questioned. If it had been the seeming clerk on 'his' own the stranger would have been challenged long ago, but Will had a look and bearing that argued he was used to being in such places, and he rode with such confidence that the few hands in the crop fields who had seen them decided they were on some kind of important business and left them alone. But now a man came out of the main building who had an outdoor look about him – he wore trail clothing, hard-wearing grey denim jeans, a woollen jacket and the traditional striped shirt.

'John Burrows,' said Philo with a little hope in her voice, but so low that only Will could hear above the sound of their horses' hoofs. Burrows came straight over to them and stood just in front of the heads of the two mounts.

'Howdy strangers, name of John Burrows, head hand at this here spread – how can I be of help to you, and what're your names?'

'I'm Will James,' said Will tipping his hat, 'and this here's a friend of mine, Philo Babbington. We have a little business over here, looking for a gent name of Walker.'

'What is your business?' asked Burrows, allowing a puzzled expression to flit over his rugged features. 'You from another spread?'

'We need to talk to him about some business,' said Philo.

'What's wrong with your voice mister?'

'He had an accident when he was young,' said Will briskly. 'Now, is Mister Walker around?'

'Yeah, he's there,' said Burrows, 'but he was kind of – busy last night. He's not in the mood to see anybody.'

'Well, we need to talk to him about property and money. Go mention the word "Wilder" to him, guess that'll pull his rope.' Once more Burrows looked faintly puzzled, but he turned and went back into the building. He was gone for a short while, and then he returned.

'Sure, he'll see you, but be warned, he was hitting the sauce last night.' As they dismounted and tethered their horses and began to walk into the building, Burrows started following them, but Will turned and faced him.

'Whoah, let's take it easy here. This is a private audience with this lordship, if you know what I mean?'

'Ok, but he's wary of strangers.' Burrows gave them a look askance and walked away; as overseer he was a busy man with plenty to do other than play nursemaid to his boss. Pauline watched him go with a fondness in her gaze that she could not conceal.

'John was always one of Father's best workers, he was right there when he died. I guess if I hadn't been so borne down and depressed by my circumstances I could have stayed, and faced the situation. He would have backed me to the hilt.' Her voice was low so that it would not carry into the inner sanctum. Will strode in first.

He found that he was inside the main entrance to a neo-colonial building, in a large hallway with wide central staircase that swept upwards, the stairs painted a dark shade of blue like the banisters. The floors in the lower hall were varnished in a dark brown stain. Apart from that the place was a mess, empty whiskey and gin bottles and discarded plates lying everywhere; then there was a shout from the main sitting room.

'Come in!' called a voice, and they entered, and found that this room was, if possible, even more of a mess than the hall they had just left, with everything covered in discarded debris, empty bottles on the ground and an atmosphere thickly redolent of cigar smoke. It was clear that since his return to the family home Troy Walker had been in the mood to party hard. Walker himself did not look like the clean-shaven hero type that Pauline had married. His beard had been growing and his hair was ruffled, moreover his clothes were crumpled and it was obvious that he had not taken a bath for a little while.

'Only reason you got to see me was because you mentioned Wilder.' He looked sharply from one to the other, or as sharply as his bleary, red-rimmed eyes would allow. 'You got some kind of news for me?'

'Good news,' said Will, taking the lead and lying for the first time. 'We met up with Mr Wilder, though he has been laid low by an unfortunate accident,' he held up a restraining hand to stop Walker from interrupting. 'It's all right, he's fine, but he couldn't make the journey on his own. He paid us a few dollars to take the trip, and said you would pay us a few dollars more. His news is simple enough, he said we were to let you know your problem has been dealt with. If you come to Miners' Delight you'll see for yourself, but to hurry.

Then you've to speak to the lawyer.' At the news, Walker did not exactly get up from where he half sat, half lay on the stuffed horsehair sofa, but he did sit more upright, giving a visible wince at the alcohol-induced ache in his head.

'You're sure of this?' he said.

'It's all dealt with.'

'Then this is mine, all mine,' Walker stood up with a visible effort. 'They were loyal to her, the hands, the women on the ranch estate, that's why I had to stay nearly locked in here. They had faith she would return, but now...' his voice trailed off and he stood there trembling with joy. 'I can get out of here now. You guys wait and I'll get cleaned up and ready, might take a little whiles because none of them'll obey me, but I'll go to Hamilton with you, identify the body and sign the necessary papers. Once I have the certificate I'll see the lawyers, then this is all mine to dispose of! And I'll dismiss 'em all!' he realized that he had been talking loudly, almost shouting. He was obviously still a little drunk from the night before.

He disappeared and did as he promised, but when he returned clean-shaven and more like his old self, Will was no longer standing there with Philo, the clerk, but with Pauline, Walker's wife.

*

Troy Walker gave a startled look at the wife whom he had clearly thought was dead. His wits had obviously been dulled by the debauchery of the last few days, but he would have needed to be dead not to gather what was going on. He jumped in the manner of a startled deer, and would have taken flight, but Will had produced a large, deadly looking Colt .45 with a rather worn handle, indicating that it might have been well used.

'You ain't going anywhere except where we tell you to go,' said Will.

'Where's that?' mumbled Walker, in the manner of a man who is in a living nightmare.

'Why, Pauline here has an old family lawyer in Riverton. We're going to see him, the three of us, and you're goin' to apply for a divorce straight off.'

'What if I refuse?' said Walker, straightening what was left of his spine.

'Maybe this will persuade you,' said Pauline leaning forwards and handing him a sheet of paper.

'What the hell's this?'

'It's a signed confession, signed and dated by Huck Wilder, and it shows everything you asked him to do, you coward!' she could not help adding the last two words. Walker took the piece of paper scanned it, and then ripped it into several small pieces, rapidly, with no sign of compassion.

'We got him to sign several,' said Will mildly. 'See, your wife ain't that stupid that she would give you the only copy.' He gestured with his gun, indicating the direction in which Walker was to go. Pauline had already told Will that the stables were out the back of the building. In the meantime she had transformed herself back into the clerk by piling up her hair, putting on her hat and pulling it down low, and replacing her false moustache.

'I don't want to answer any awkward questions, it's easier this way,' she said as they went to the stables, and Walker was made to saddle up, wincing as he did so, indicating that his hangover was still making its presence known. Will pulled the sleeve of his jacket down so that it all but concealed the weapon, and the three of them went to the front of the building, Walker leading his horse, a look on his face that indicated he was living a nightmare.

As the other two got on their own horses they were careful to keep him in the middle.

'I know you from when we went out together riding in the hills, you're not that good a horseman, Troy.' She pulled aside her waistcoat and showed him a pearl-handed Colt in a holster at her side. 'If you try to get away I'll shoot you. I won't kill you, but you'll be in a lot of pain.' Walker looked around desperately, but he knew that here, of all places, there was little in the way of help. Besides, a ranch was a busy place and most of the hands were at work riding out, herding and dealing with the animals.

They rode at a sedate pace towards the outskirts of the Ryder spread, with Pauline dictating the pace and Walker saying nothing, which was remarkable considering how glib he was in normal life, while Will was not a man who said much anyway.

They were approaching the trail towards Riverton when they heard the sound of a horse's hoofs behind them, approaching fast. Pauline looked back and saw with a sense of relief that they were being followed by John Burrows.

'Hey!' he called as he came closer, 'Where are you going, Mr Walker?'

'Got some business in town,' said Walker. Burrows rode closer to them, right up beside Walker. Pauline felt a sense of relief, perhaps she could even show who she was.

'I was working with the cattle when one of the hands told me that you were making off with these two,' said Burrows. 'Is everything OK?'

'Fine,' said Walker, 'just going into town for a little business, be back later,' but his tone was that of a man who was going to be hanged in the morning,

'What's going on here?' asked Burrows sharply, 'you left without even a gun, what are these two up to?' This was a little too much for Pauline, and once more she revealed who she was.

'John, I'm in disguise because – well, it would take too long – but I'm back, and I'm getting this man out of my life.'

'Miss Ryder?' Burrows looked at her in astonishment. The horses were almost at a halt by now. Pauline smiled at her father's trusted head hand.

'John, we're settling this and I'll be back soon, you don't even need to come with us, everything's in hand.'

There was little distance between Burrows and Walker at this point. Burrows urged his steed around so the two men were looking at each other.

'Is this true?' he asked. Troy Walker nodded, seemingly lost for words for almost the first time in his life. Then Burrows pulled out two guns and threw one to Walker, who showed an unexpected degree of manual dexterity by catching the weapon, digging in his spurs, heeling his horse around and facing Will, pointing the barrel towards him. By this time Will had his own weapon pointed solidly at Walker. The only problem was that after tossing the weapon to Walker, Burrows also spurred his own horse and he now had his gun pointed at Will's head.

'Drop it mister,' he said, meaning that Will had no choice but to obey, and the gun thudded to the soil below. Burrows looked at Pauline.

'Real sorry about this,' he said, 'but I've been promised a real good reward, five years wages when the ranch gets sold – I can start a good life in the city.'

Walker looked at them and his twisted features were no longer handsome.

'Kill them,' he said.

*

An average person facing up to the fact that he has a gun close to his head will feel a range of emotions, from simple fear to terror at the prospect of losing their life to the impact of a forceful close-range bullet. But Will James was not the average person. He had lived most of his life using his wits, and he was used to being in situations that would have left the average man gibbering with fright.

Will had dropped his gun at his feet, and he dropped to the ground beside the weapon grabbing it with the speed of a striking rattlesnake, head, and instead of trying to fire at his enemy from an awkward angle, he placed a couple of bullets in the ground near the hoofs of the foreman's horse. The animal was not trained to deal with this kind of event because the shots kicked up a lot of dust and made a great deal of noise, and it gave a loud whickering sound, reared up and spun away sharply from the source of its fear. This had the dramatic effect of throwing off Burrows who had been holding the reins with one hand and aiming his weapon with the other.

Will was not the kind of man to hesitate when a situation turned to his advantage. He quickly threw himself off his horse and on to the man on the ground, who had dropped his gun, and punched him several times with bony fists that offered no respite. Burrows gave a grunt of surprise and pain, his head falling to one side as he was knocked unconscious.

Will had taken the risk of leaping off and attacking Burrows because he knew that his horse was between him and the traitorous coward Troy Walker.

His ploy had succeeded to the extent that he had been able to get rid of one enemy, but Walker was a better rider than he seemed, and he had moved the head of his mount so that he was facing the man on the ground.

'You're spoiling everything,' shouted Walker, completely losing his usual poise, his face twisted, red and ugly. He raised the weapon that he had been thrown by the unconscious man and aimed squarely at Will's breast. 'Die, you bastard,' he said.

'Fire that weapon and I'll blow your brains out,' said a calm female voice behind him. From where he was

Will could see that Pauline was behind their mutual enemy, and she was holding the pearl-handled pistol at the back of Walker's head. It was obvious from the way the weapon was held that she knew exactly what she was doing.

Walker gave a grimace, knowing that he could have taken the chance and fired anyway, but he was the kind of person who would rather stay alive than take revenge on his enemy. He gave a groan of despair and dropped the gun.

'It was worth a try,' he said, with a faint return to his old cockiness.

'Looks like we got two prisoners,' said Will, 'Hell, this is goin' to be a long trip.'

'Watch out,' yelled Pauline. Will was standing with his back to the fallen Burrows, but it seemed that Burrows was tough, and more cunning than he appeared. He might have received some blows that would have knocked out the average man, but he was a fit, rangy trail rider and used to taking on some rough conditions. He jumped to his feet and leapt on Will's back, bearing him forwards and to the ground.

Walker responded to this by heeling his horse around and facing the woman who was still his wife.

'This ain't finished, put the gun down and we'll show some mercy, you little bitch.' He was snarling at her now. 'By all rights this spread is mine. The minute the old guy passed I should have been the owner!'

In the meantime Will had shaken off his attacker and they rolled over in the dust, and it was obvious that they were fighting to end it all. Burrows was struggling to get to his weapon that lay close to where the two of them were battling. This was a distraction for the girl, who saw what was happening and aimed her gun at Burrows, tears streaming down her cheeks, but before she could fire, Walker, who was looking for his chance, rode his horse towards her and grabbed her wrist instead of the weapon. He pushed her arm up so that when she fired, the shot went into the air. He wrenched her arm and she gave a cry of pain, and the pistol dropped from her nerveless fingers.

Will realized what was going on, but he could not help her because he was dealing with his own problems. Burrows was within an ace of getting hold of the Colt lying on the alkaline soil of the trail. Once he did this, he would have the upper hand again. Will knew that his own gun was lying around there somewhere, since he had dropped it when he had jumped on the gunman.

While scrabbling for the weapon Burrows left his back exposed, so Will did something that he had not done for many years – and it was one of the most effective moves if carried out properly – he aimed his boot and kicked his opponent right up the backside. The force of the blow was such that it had immediate effect. Burrows promptly forgot about the weapon and gave a deep groan that was torn from deep inside his body. He arched his back, tried to stand up, and fell to the ground in pain, flopping around like a newly landed fish.

Will ignored him and snatched up the weapon, looked wildly around and saw his own gun. He shoved the first one in his belt, grabbed his own, which he holstered. He ran over to where Walker was still grappling with Pauline. Walker had nearly unseated her from the horse.

'Let her go,' said Will, reinforcing his words by grabbing Walker's jacket and giving a forceful heave. Walker gave a wild shout, was unseated and fell to the ground with an almighty thump. Will had a few strong blows left in those bony fists. Faced with a winded Walker he made a few blows directed to the head and body and Walker hit the dust, one man who was not going to rise again for a while.

'Are you all right?' Will asked Pauline. She was holding her injured arm, but her eyes were shining as she smiled at him through her tears.

'I am now,' she said.

THIRTEEN

SWEET JUSTICE

Obadiah Palmer was sitting at his desk when Will James knocked and came into the office after the door was opened by one of the deputies.

'You don't just let people walk in the door?' asked Will.

'Nope,' said the sheriff, 'when people in a town walk around with guns as a matter of course, sometimes they decide they've got a grudge and reckon I'm the object of that grudge and try to blow my head off'a my shoulders. It's easier just to wait and see who's there – but I'm guessing you ain't here to talk about office politics.' He got up from behind his desk and looked up to his former suspect.

'The circuit judge has been, Tunnock was found guilty of conspiracy and sent to prison for a few years, and Gandon received a similar sentence. I told them the investigation into Grundy's death was closed when it was seen that it was a straightforward case of self-defence. But again, you ain't here to discuss a decision that's been ratified and stowed away, you're here about what happened between you and the little lady.'

'The truth was something Pauline couldn't see,' said James. 'Guess she was a little too close to what was happening. Her father's foreman, John Burrows, was part of the conspiracy to take away her ranch. He and Walker knew that the old man wasn't in the best of health, and Walker had to work fast and get in with the girl so they would be married before the old guy met his maker. Trouble was, Walker hadn't bothered to check the law of the land, which was different from the law Texas, where he came from. When her father passed away Walker discovered that *she* was the legal owner of the entire spread, so of course he reacted like all spoiled brats, and became moody and violent. Burrows wasn't there because he was away dealing with business, but she got a message to him, then copped out of the whole deal by vanishing. I guess she thought Burrows would suppress Walker so that she could return in due course, but they were in league the whole time.'

'So what happened to you out there, Will?'

'Well, he and Burrows gave themselves away and attacked us both. We overcame them and took them off to Riverton, where they're both currently languishing in jail, the sheriff there having known Pauline's family for years. As for the law with regard to her marriage, it was a false marriage for gain, and the family lawyer – who had innocently told Walker already that he needed to prove his wife was dead before he could inherit – has said that he will have the marriage annulled within days.'

Will looked around the gaol, and realized for the first time that the deputy – who had other business – had left, and that the two of them were alone in the building.

'Wait a minute, there's a prisoner missing, ain't there? What happened to Wilder?'

'He's dead,' said the sheriff. 'Son-of-a-bitch had been in a fight, had a head wound and was in a pretty bad way when he came down here with Betsy and Old Brand, with a signed confession. You and Pauline had already gone by then, and the circuit judge had left, so I imprisoned him for the next time. One of his head wounds turned bad and his breathing got real short, and he died a day or so later,' he shrugged. 'It happens, but I still have his confession, I guess that's going to be an important part of how I report what happened.'

Will thrust out one of his big, work-roughened hands, grabbed the sheriff's somewhat plumper one, and shook it vigorously.

'I think I have you to thank for everything sheriff. You believed in me, and that's all a man needs.'

'You weren't the only reason,' said Palmer, and at that precise moment there was a knock at the door. Palmer answered, and Pauline came in, looking feminine and pretty in her new summer dress, her long hair brushed and burnished to dark gold. 'She's the other,' said Palmer.

The young, pretty woman dispensed with all courtesy and gave the sheriff the warmest hug he had ever known.

'You're the whole reason we're here,' she said, 'except for the girls at the store. I went to see them and told them the truth about "Philo". One of them, Emmaline, was cut up because she had led me into danger; she told me how she had known Wilder, but that he had died. Is that right?'

'Yep,' said Palmer, who was still recovering from the hug.

'I would never kill anyone,' said Pauline, 'but he was a horrible man, and I don't know how many lives he had helped to destroy.'

'He's better off where he is,' said Palmer. 'Saves the bother of a hangin'.' He smiled at them both and watched as they left, the big man with his easy, swinging stride and the dainty, pretty woman at his side, who, when they were some distance away, grabbed Will's hand as they walked.

And the sheriff smiled.

*

Betsy was in her father's guest house, alone and feeling a little deflated.

Her visitors had gone and she had wished them all the best for their future life together, and now she would be here for the rest of her natural days, because out here, she would never meet the right person, and she would never, for the rest of her days, tell Pauline that she had harboured secret hopes for a romance with Will James.

There was a knock on the front door. Betsy was wearing the apron she put on for cooking the mid-day meal;

she answered the door wearing this, and found that she was looking at Billy Birch. Birch was dressed in what could only be described as Sunday finery and was clean-shaven, unlike the last time she had seen him when he was in work clothes, and part of the lynch party carrying a thick rope. This time he was holding nothing more than a box of chocolates, which he had bought in the new department store in town from a charming assistant called Emmaline.

'I'll get my father,' said Betsy, but Billy took off his soft brown felt hat with one hand, and handed the box of chocolates to her with a flourish with the other. She was so surprised that she took them.

'Listen, I know we got off to a bad start, but I realize I was wrong to let Oregon Pete mislead me. He was just real sore about losing young Josh. I was so affected by how you stood up for that young man, Philo, that when I thought it over it broke my heart.'

'Did it really?' But she did not smile.

'I work hard,' he said, 'I got a lot to offer, but I knowed Grundy was after you. I needed the business he put my way, so I took the coward's way out, but I always thought you was real nice, Betsy. Just give me a chance, that's all I ask.'

'I shouldn't,' she said, 'but you listened to Will and you left. You've taken all this trouble to be here, so come in and talk – but my father will be here the whole time.'

'That's fine by me,' said Billy. She turned away and walked invitingly inside the building, holding the chocolates. He could no longer see her face, but this time she was smiling.